In spring, the road lead[...] trees of pale-green bu[...] becomes a leafy tunn[...] splashes, winding its way towards the village. Along the coast, overhanging trees tilt above the sea and ancient roots swirl in the incoming tide. These tangled woodlands are all that is left of a vast forest land that was once called Trá na Coille.

In those far-off days, it was a wild, lonely place. Families fished along its coast. Farmers cleared the land and built their settlements from the strong oak wood. In medieval times, King Henry II granted the forests and a royal title to an officer from Bristol, James Hobourne. A castle was built and trees were felled to create a rich, pastoral estate for Lord and Lady Hobourne.

As the centuries passed, Trá na Coille became Beachwood. The trees continued to be felled, their strong timbers furnishing fine houses and mighty warships. Its population farmed and fished and traded, or they worked on the Hobourne estate which was located to the north of Dublin city. In 1970, the Hobourne family sold their lands and home to the Irish Government. Hobourne House became the local secondary school. Land was sold for development and housing estates were built with names like Oaktree, Cypress, Elmgrove and Ashwood. The gardens and grounds were turned into a public park. The population grew, and in Hobourne Park, young people began to gather in Fountain Square.

Today it is their favourite meeting spot. Ask them about Beachwood and they will tell you that it is a magic place with the sea and the city and the country all rolled up together. But during the winter months, when the trees form a bleak guard-of-honour and the grey sea lashes the coast, they will complain that it is Drearsville, on the edge of nowhere. I would like to introduce you to these young people as they move through the seasons. Join them on their good days and their bad days. Dance and play, fight, grieve, love and laugh with them. But most of all, enjoy them.

SUMMER AT FOUNTAIN SQUARE

BEACHWOOD

SUMMER AT FOUNTAIN SQUARE

JUNE CONSIDINE

POOLBEG

First published 1993 by
Poolbeg Press Ltd
Knocksedan House,
Swords, Co Dublin, Ireland

© June Considine 1993

The moral right of the author has been asserted.

A catalogue record for this book is available from the British Library.

ISBN 1 85371 261 2

Cover design by Pomphrey Associates
Cover illustration by Brian Caffrey
Set by Mac Book Limited in Stone 9.5/13
Printed by Cox & Wyman,
Reading, Berks

Cast of Characters

Young People
Danny Kane
Lorraine Crowe
Gary Crowe, her elder brother
Joanne Tully
Amanda Bell
Marian Lambert
Robbie Finlay
Jason Cole
Caro Kane, Danny's younger sister
Jennifer Hilliard

Young people who gather at Fountain Square

Adults
Zena Crowe, mother of Lorraine and Gary and
                      proprietor of The Zany Crowe's Nest
Jeff Crowe, father of Lorraine and Gary and lead
                          guitarist with Vulture's Dawn
John Donaldson, artist
Stinger Muldoon, fisherman
Larry, builder
Brendan, plasterer
Fr O'Beirne, original parish priest
Fr Cowan, new parish priest
Mrs Corr, church cleaner
Mr Boylan (The Boil), park keeper

Dogs
Candy, Lorraine's dog
Beethoven, Stinger's dog
Rachmaninov, Jonathan Kane's dog

Danny's Groups
Dancing on Grey Ash
The Flame of the Passion

Staff at The Zany Crowe's Nest Restaurant
Jack, chef
Roderick, wine waiter
Fiona, waitress

Locations

Fountain Square
The Zany Crowe's Nest Restaurant
Harbour Bend
White Light Studio
Baymeadow Dump
Rockfield Heights
St Teresa's Church
World United Cinemas, nicknamed "The WUC"

*To my nephew and niece Neil and
Deirdre O'Connor*

Chapter One

For as long as Danny Kane could remember, he had known that he was going to be a rock star. At school, his desk was a piano. While teachers talked about simple and compound interest, his fingers tapped over the keys, composing rock operas and rhapsodies in rap. When they outlined battle dates, rebellions and uprisings, he played upon his imaginary drum. As pupils groaned under the weight of prose and poetry, Danny's lips shaped lyrics that would right the wrongs of the world and take the music industry by storm.

He dismissed his mother's worries about drink, drugs and sex with an indulgent laugh. Those temptations were for lesser humans. He was going to sing about environmental wrongdoings and develop an image, ozone-friendly and green-clean.

When Danny was twelve, U2 were a big Irish influence on him. For his birthday, his father bought him a Bono hat. Although it kept falling over his eyebrows, he wore it everywhere. His friends teased him and called him a poser. It was confiscated three times in school. Then Gary Crowe grabbed it from him one night at the Beachwood youth club, and ran off, waving it in the air like a flag. The following day, it was discovered on the head of the statue of St Bernadette. From her vantage point at the foot of Our Lady's grotto in the grounds of St Teresa's church, the little statue with the upturned face wore it with quiet dignity.

"Beachwood brats!" hissed Mrs Corr, the woman who cleaned the church. "Gurriers, every one of them. No respect for the blessed saint and even less for my poor arthritic bones." She climbed over the rocks surrounding St Bernadette and removed the hat. Balanced on top of her sweeping brush, it was grimly carried across the road to the house of Fr O'Beirne, the parish priest of Beachwood.

The following day, Fr O'Beirne addressed the sixth class pupils of St Teresa's Primary School. He lectured them about respect for property, all property, but especially for the sacred property of the Lord.

"I shall look forward to meeting the owner of this Beano hat in my presbytery this evening." Fr O'Beirne finished his lecture on this ominous note.

Danny gulped and cursed the back of Gary Crowe's neck.

"It's a Bono hat," said Joanne Tully, trying not to giggle. "It's to do with U2, Father!"

"Me too!" barked the priest. His eyes glinted as he surveyed the rows of pupils. They shuffled their feet and gazed at the wall above his head. "What do you mean, me too? I had no part to play in this silly prank. Did you?"

"Oh, no, Father," said Joanne, blushing and sliding down in her desk, wondering if the parish priest was laughing at her.

Danny had no intention of calling on Fr O'Beirne. But the thought of his precious hat sitting on the shiny table in the presbytery was more than he could stand. He took a deep breath and rang the bell.

The priest was an old man with a ruddy, plump face and bright blue eyes. Despite his age, he was pretty clued in to what went on in Beachwood. He had noticed Danny, plus his hat, on a number of occasions and had also heard him play his guitar at the school Christmas concerts.

"A folk mass for teenagers," said Fr O'Beirne. "That's what I'm trying to organise. I'm tired of you youngsters killing time on the steps of the church every Sunday while I'm inside doing my utmost to get the Lord to see you through the coming week." He paused for breath. "This praying lark, it's not that easy, you know. I need a bit of help now and again. So, how about it, Danny? Will you join my folk group?"

"But I'm not a teenager," gasped Danny, horrified. "I'm only twelve!" He would die if he had to stand on the altar steps, strumming his guitar with all his friends grinning up at him from the front row.

"No matter," said Fr O'Beirne. "There's no age limit on genius and I know you're deadly when you get a guitar into your hands."

"That's not true," insisted Danny. "I'm terrible. Awful!"

"Nonsense, my boy." The priest had tilted the Bono hat over Danny's eyes. "I'm highly qualified to recognise a gift from the Lord when I hear it. And you've got good music in your fingers. Just keep the knees from rocking and rolling, won't you? We can't have that sort of carry-on on the altar. See you at rehearsals on Wednesday."

The future rock star opened his mouth to protest. But

Fr O'Beirne had suddenly developed a hard-of-hearing problem and kept saying, "Yes, that's right, my boy. Seven-thirty Wednesday evening and don't forget your guitar."

Danny could not believe it. He was to become the lead guitarist and singer in a folk group called The Flame of the Passion. His first gig, far from being performed in a smoky, vibrating rock club as he had hoped, was about to be launched from the altar steps of St Teresa's Church.

When Caroline Kane (known to her friends as Caro) heard that her brother had become part of a folk group called The Flame of the Passion, she decided that he should have his own fan-club. Caro was only ten at the time but she watched *Top of the Pops* every Thursday night and knew that a star was nothing without a full-throated and devoted following.

On the first Sunday that Danny played lead guitar and sang with The Flame of the Passion, ten young girls sat in the front row and swayed soulfully to the rhythm of his music. Afterwards, he had a dreadful row with his younger sister.

"Get rid of them," he ordered. "Get them out of my life or I'll never speak to you again."

"No can do," replied Caro. "I can't control them any longer." She sounded like a zoo keeper who had accidentally unlocked the cage door on a pride of wild lions. "There's twice as many coming along next Sunday."

"Then I'll stop them. I won't let them in!" roared Danny.

"But you can't turn them away from the doors of God's house!" Caro was triumphant and self-righteous. "That would be a terrible thing to do."

Danny spluttered and wondered what his life would

be like if Caro had never been born. Without a doubt, his road to stardom would be a whole lot easier.

The first few Sundays were dreadful. He tried to ignore the front row which held his proud family, his fan-club and his grinning classmates. Gary Crowe kept conducting him and miming opera singers until he was sharply nudged by an old woman called Mrs Maxwell, who had a ferociously cross expression on her face.

The fan-club ringleaders were Caro and her three friends, Aoife Johnston, Jennifer Hilliard and Emma Patton. Emma was Church of Ireland but she became an honorary Catholic for an hour every Sunday, just to hear Danny play. Between them, they encouraged other girls to come along and the number of enthusiastic fans increased. They swayed to the music of The Flame of the Passion and burst into applause at the end of mass. Fr O'Beirne was forced to make a rule. No Danny Kane fan was to sit further than half-way up the church, unless accompanied by an adult.

With his fans reduced to craning their necks from the centre of the church, Danny discovered that he actually enjoyed being part of the folk group. Sometimes his individual style of playing caused trouble. Once he did a guitar solo in the middle of the Lord's Prayer. This threw Fr O'Beirne off his stride so much that he forgot the prayers that followed and had to be prompted by Katie, the altar girl. Gradually, Danny's friends stopped teasing him.

As Fr O'Beirne had hoped, the steps of the church were no longer crowded with listless teenagers and Danny began to enjoy what he called "his Sunday morning gig." He stayed with The Flame of the Passion until he was fifteen.

Everyone in Beachwood was shocked that April when Fr O'Beirne died suddenly from a heart attack. As he had requested, he was buried in St Teresa's churchyard. His funeral was simple and his beloved folk group played at his graveside. They wondered how the new parish priest would react to their music.

They soon found out. Fr Cowan was a tone-deaf, burly man with a furrowed forehead and a low line in tolerance. He shuddered his way through ten-thirty Mass. When Danny sang and played his own composition, "Heavenly Rave," the priest raised horrified eyes to the crucifix above the altar. After Mass, the young musicians were told that The Flame of the Passion was being disbanded.

Danny's brief claim to fame was at an end. Yet his fans continued to hang like troublesome, devoted albatrosses around his neck. They wanted to listen to him every Sunday morning and planned the most brilliant protest schemes to bring this about. Danny lived in constant dread of what they intended doing. He woke up sweating one night from a nightmare in which they had placed him in a candlestick on the altar and Aoife Johnston was trying to set his hair on fire.

At the start of the school summer holidays Fr Cowan rang Danny one morning and ordered him to report to the entrance of the church where the daily ten o'clock Mass had just ended.

"But...but...why?" gasped Danny.

In reply, the priest held the receiver away from his ear. Danny heard a strange sound.

"Do you know what that is?" demanded Fr Cowan.

"Is it a mad dog barking?" asked Danny.

"An understandable mistake." Fr Cowan was breathing very heavily. "It is the horrible sound of a group of chanting young girls who claim to belong to the Danny Kane fan-club. They are currently involved in a protest outside my church and I would like them removed. Immediately!"

Danny moaned softly. But Fr Cowan had already hung up.

The chanting sound reached his ears as the church spire came into view. A number of young teenagers (to Danny's horrified eyes it looked like hundreds) were walking in a large circle and carrying placards. Caro was holding one of the biggest placards with a message in orange paint that read: *Don't Quench the Passionate Flame*. The letters had wavering lines coming from them at different angles so that they looked like flames. Jennifer Hilliard had another luridly-painted message. *A Passionate Plea to Fr Cowan! Save the Flames*.

"Ah, Danny. The man of the moment!" Fr Cowan growled. A large crowd had gathered to watch the action. "As you seem to have been the main attraction in The Flame of the Passion, perhaps you could persuade these young ladies to leave peacefully. Otherwise I shall have to use my full powers of authority and the flames that will result from that encounter will never be quenched!" With this last threat Fr Cowan left the protesters and retired to his church to pray for patience.

"Hey, Danny! I've told Fr Cowan I'm becoming a Hare Krishna if he doesn't bring back The Flames." This information was shouted at him by Jennifer who then led the chant, "We're aflame—for Danny Kane."

A quick glance around showed that the crowd had swelled in numbers. Some of his friends had arrived. They whistled and clapped and encouraged the fans to chant even louder.

"We're aflame—for Danny Kane." His screaming fans obliged.

"Shut up!" Danny yelled and clutched his head.

They stopped and stared at him from hurt eyes.

"We're doing this for your sake, Danny," explained his sister. "We're trying to save your career."

"But I'm moving on to bigger and better things," said Danny.

"Such as?" shouted Emma.

"I'm…I'm forming a new group." This was news to Danny as well as to his fans. But suddenly it seemed like a wonderful idea.

Aoife did not believe him. "Rubbish! You're only making that up! We want The Flame of the Passion!" The fans were thoroughly enjoying themselves and were not going to be fobbed off with feeble excuses.

Danny held up his hands, palms towards them in a begging gesture. "I'll give you all complimentary tickets to my first gig," he promised. "And I'll dedicate my first album to you."

He noticed a girl leaning on the handlebars of a bicycle. She was wearing cycling shorts and a T-shirt, a tanned and leggy girl with fine blonde hair tied back in a French plait.

Unable to cycle through the crowd, she had stopped to watch the action. Tears of laughter ran down her face and she gave Danny a wide, sympathetic grin. When his fans prepared to resume their chant, she cupped her hands to her mouth and shouted, "Sergeant Hilliard is on his way. I just saw him getting into the squad car."

A loud groan arose from fans and onlookers alike.

"Oh no! Hide me! Hide me!" wailed Jennifer, ducking behind Danny.

Sergeant Hilliard was feared by all the teenagers in Beachwood. They normally ran in the opposite direction whenever they saw him but, as he was Jennifer's father, she was denied this escape route.

"We'd better cool it!" someone yelled in panicked tones.

"We have a right to protest!" Caro tried to hold the fans together. But, suddenly, Danny was a lost cause and the fans marched off, still carrying their placards, still chanting until they rounded the corner of Church Road.

"Thanks a million!" Danny walked over to the blonde girl. "Those girls! I can't believe they'd pull such a stroke. Did you really see Sergeant Hilliard?"

"Oh yes." She blushed and gave him a shy smile. "But he was being driven in the opposite direction."

Danny burst out laughing and mopped his forehead. The girl joined in. She was about his own age and looked vaguely familiar. He tried to remember if he had seen her at the leisure centre, the youth club, or with the crowd who hung out in Fountain Square.

"What's your name?" he asked.

"Lorraine Crowe."

"Oh!" Danny's voice sounded flat. He remembered her from primary school. How quiet she had been in those days, pale and shy, with limp hair falling over her face, always alone and walking close to walls as if she was afraid of getting in anyone's way. She had also been extremely clever and had been branded a swot by her classmates.

"You're Gary Crowe's sister?" Gary was not his favourite person.

"Guilty." Her eyes were on the pedals of her bike. The colour deepened in her cheeks.

It was obvious to Danny that, despite her show of confidence in front of the fans, she was still a very shy person.

"I haven't seen you around much, lately."

"I go to boarding school now, so I'm only here during the holidays." She steadied her bike and prepared to cycle away.

"Do you ever go to Fountain Square?" He tried to detain her.

"No. I'm not really part of the crowd that hang out there." She sounded wistful.

"Why don't you come tomorrow? I'm taking the guitar along." He sounded casual yet there was a persuasive undercurrent to his words.

"Maybe I will."

"See you then."

She bent her head over the handlebars and did not reply.

In the dim, candle-lit church, Fr Cowan raised his eyes to the altar and cried: "Dear Lord, I know that I asked you to send me on a difficult and demanding mission. But why did you have to send me to Beachwood?"

Chapter Two

L orraine Crowe had been four years old when her father left home. Eleven years later, she found it impossible to remember his face but sometimes, when she allowed her mind to go very quiet, she would recall the sound of music. It always faded away, to be replaced by shrill, angry voices and slamming doors.

Mrs Crowe never talked about her husband. If Lorraine asked questions, her mother always looked so cross and troubled that the words fell into a guilty silence.

"Jeff was a musician, an idler and a dreamer," said Aunt Olive, his sister, who lived in Dalkey and was fond of plain speaking. Her brother had been lead guitarist with a rock group called Vulture's Dawn when he met a young woman called Zena Pearson. She was ambitious and hard-working. He wanted nothing more from life than to play his guitar and become a star. Their friends said: "It will never last!" and danced at their wedding a year later.

When Gary was born, Zena talked to her husband

11

about getting a steady job. He talked about getting the right breaks, making the right contacts, being in the right place at the right time. Eighteen months later, Lorraine was born. This time, Zena discussed their future in a hard, determined voice and Jeff promised to give up playing his guitar. Soon afterwards, he began working with a company called Bricken and Brace Exports. Vulture's Dawn found a new lead guitarist and Jeff Crowe stayed home at night. He had the haunted look of a man who sees his future stretching before him in a narrow, boring line.

As the fame of Vulture's Dawn grew, so did Jeff Crowe's envy and discontent. He wanted to give up his job and take a new band on the road. Lorraine figured that that was the time of the shrill voices and slamming doors.

"Row after row," agreed Aunt Olive. She said that his music was like an addiction and whenever he met any of his musician friends, he would spend all night playing guitar with them.

When the lead guitarist with Vulture's Dawn left just before a major European tour, Jeff Crowe was asked to rejoin. The house seemed to clang with his wife's anger. She banged saucepans on the cooker and cutlery on the table to drown out his voice.

"Our marriage or your music! You must choose," she told him. He begged her to understand. He needed one final musical fling. In six weeks time he would be home again and he would find another steady job.

"No, you won't," she replied and turned her face away when he tried to kiss her goodbye. A strange, waiting silence followed his departure. It was the beginning of the end of their marriage. A year later, when Vulture's

Dawn went on an American tour, Jeff went with them and did not return to Ireland. Lorraine only heard her mother weeping once and the sound was so awful that she buried her head under the bedclothes and pressed her pillow to her ears. In the blackness that surrounded her, she allowed her father's face to fade away.

Zena Crowe was young and determined. She had made a mistake but she would erase it forever by proving that she did not need a weak and selfish husband. "Life is too short to be wasted on anything other than excellence," she announced, and with this motto, she set about rebuilding her life.

She borrowed money from the bank and opened her own business, a small sandwich bar. It specialised in home-made herb breads and delicious, unusual fillings. She called it Zany Spreads. Zany was the nickname her father had given her when she was a child.

Five years after the opening of the first sandwich bar, there were five highly successful Zany Spreads operating around Dublin. Lorraine was ten years old when her mother sold the sandwich bars and moved her family from Sandymount to Beachwood, a small village north of Dublin. She opened a posh restaurant called The Zany Crowe's Nest. Within a short time, this was the place to eat in Beachwood Village.

Vulture's Dawn no longer existed. Lorraine's father was still playing his guitar and following a pathful of dreams. She never replied to his letters. After a while they stopped, although they continued to arrive for Gary. His mother never asked him questions about the contents. He told Lorraine that their father was singing and playing in a nightclub and had changed his name to Caley Jones. On two occasions, Gary had travelled to New York with his Aunt Olive and visited his father. The same silence greeted his return. It was as if Jeff Crowe, with his dreams and his music, had never existed.

But Gary was unable to let his mother forget. He had pleaded with her to buy him a guitar and let him attend guitar lessons. She refused. He sulked and argued. It made no difference. His problem, said his mother, was that he always wanted his own way and was too wrapped up in himself to care about anyone else. Lorraine knew that what her mother was really saying was that Gary was like his father. But those words would never be uttered.

When Lorraine was fourteen and on her school holidays, she answered a ring on their doorbell one evening. She recognised Jem Howard, the ex-drummer with Vulture's Dawn.

He looked relieved when he heard that Mrs Crowe was out. On his holidays in New York he had met their father. "He hasn't changed a bit. Still chasing the same dream and always the same two paces behind it."

Lorraine always got a tight feeling around her heart whenever her father's name was mentioned. But Gary was hanging on to every word. Jem handed him a guitar-case and a letter. The letter fell to the ground when Gary opened the case and stared at the guitar.

"That's the same one he used to play when he was living here," he blurted out and cast a quick, guilty look towards a portrait of his mother hanging above the fireplace. Lorraine picked up the letter. He sent his love to them both and wanted to know why Lorraine never answered his letters. He was anxious to pass something he treasured on to his children and hoped that Lorraine remembered the times he had played his guitar for her when she was a baby.

Gary ran his fingers over the guitar strings, as if defying the painted eyes of the portrait that seemed to gaze down upon him with chilly disapproval. Jem rubbed his hands together when Lorraine offered him a glass of whiskey. "A tough woman, your mother. Better not to tell her I called, eh?"

"Don't worry," Gary said without any expression whatsoever in his voice. "We won't." He glared at Lorraine. "Don't you dare open your mouth about this or you're in deep trouble," he warned.

"I'm not a sneak," she retorted. She had a strong desire to take her father's letter and crumple it into the refuse bin. Out of sight, out of mind. "You'll be in trouble if she finds out that you're keeping that guitar."

"So what's new!" Gary scowled.

He was always in trouble for something or other. Bad report cards, mitching from school, having to stay back an extra year in primary school because of bad grades, staying out late, messing up his room, smoking, being cheeky. The rows between Gary and his mother were so repetitive that Lorraine could frame the words before they were ever uttered.

"Study, study, study! That's all you ever think about," Gary would shout. "Even when I do the best I can, it's never enough. You're never satisfied!"

"That's right! I demand a high standard and I expect my children to deliver. Lorraine fulfils my expectations through hard work and effort. Why can't you do the same?"

Gary would glance scornfully at his sister. "We all know why she's a swot. She hasn't got a single friend. What else does she have to do with her time except study?"

"If you decided to take a leaf from her book, it would serve you a lot better than making fun of her. You want everything in life handed to you on a plate without making any effort to earn it!"

Lorraine would feel like shouting: "Stop it, both of you! Why can't you listen to each other instead of using words to hit each other all the time."

Those rows and her brother's scorn were Lorraine's reasons for going to boarding school. When she first moved to Beachwood, Lorraine had become friendly with Joanne Tully, who was in her class. But Gary told her that everyone, including Joanne, said she was a boring swot and laughed at her behind her back. Gary was right when he called her a swot. Lorraine had no problem with that word. She did not understand why he made it sound like some sort of social disease. Liz O'Rourke was brilliant at tennis and spent all her spare time playing at Beachwood Tennis Club. Danny Kane loved music and spent all his free time playing his guitar. Lorraine enjoyed studying and achieving good results. It was the same challenge that attracted Liz to the net and Danny to music. But no one considered their interests boring or dull. Gary said that that was because they weren't boring or dull whereas one only had to look at Lorraine to know that she was all of those things.

Lorraine believed him. Every time she saw Joanne laughing with Amanda Bell or any of the other girls in her class, she was convinced they were making fun of her. She put on a snooty face and began to ignore Joanne, who was too popular to worry for long about her new friend's off-hand behaviour.

Lorraine knew that if her confidence was to develop she needed to be away from Gary. John Donaldson, a family friend and the artist who had painted the portrait of her mother, agreed and had suggested Iona Abbey to Mrs Crowe.

Things were different in Iona Abbey. Lorraine had made friends and felt a deep satisfaction when her teachers praised her grades and her skill on the debating team. But Gary could still make her feel awkward and ugly and boring, no matter how much she tried to ignore him.

Whenever his mother was out of the house, Gary played his father's guitar in his room. Every time she came home on holidays Lorraine noticed the improvement in his playing. If her mother found out! Her heart gave an anxious little quiver when she thought about the row that would follow.

Then she scolded herself, firmly. It was not her business. Let them fight! She was on her summer holidays and had made a solemn vow to start hanging out in Fountain Square. To make friends again with Joanne Tully. To get to know Danny Kane. Yesterday, he had asked her to go to Fountain Square. Even thinking about it made her breath quicken. Candy, her golden collie, barked with excitement when she saw her lead. She had beautiful ears and a silky coat, the colour of molten gold. Lorraine had only reached her gate when Bells' front door opened and Amanda came running down the driveway. She lived in the house directly opposite the Crowes.

"Hi, Lorraine. Are you going for a walk?"

"Yes." Reluctantly, Lorraine waited until the girl crossed the road.

Amanda had a round face and cropped black hair. Her eyes narrowed and her smile was falsely bright when she said, "Gary says you're getting too stuck-up to talk to us since you went to that posh boarding school."

"Of course I'm not." Lorraine squirmed with embarrassment.

"I suppose you sailed through your Junior Cert—not like poor me. It must be great to be so clever." Amanda laughed a laugh that said "poor unfortunate swot."

"No, I didn't. It was horrendous!" protested Lorraine, although she had found this national examination done by all third year students quite easy. She disliked Amanda and the coy way she praised people to their faces and said horrible things about them behind their backs.

Amanda leaned closer. "Joanne's going to be in the doghouse when the results come out. She's sure she failed maths and her father's going to freak. I told her that she should have stopped running around with Danny Kane and tried studying for a change. But I don't think she was listening."

"Are they going together?" Lorraine asked. She wished that Candy would not keep jumping up and down with impatience.

Amanda smirked. "She's nuts about him, has been for ages. I don't know what she sees in him. He's a real poser, the way he goes around with that guitar all the time. He deliberately got those stupid fans of his to go and protest outside the church. My mother says it's a disgrace and an insult to Fr Cowan."

"I liked that group," said Lorraine. "It was a mistake to break them up. Danny Kane is a very good guitarist."

Amanda's pale-blue eyes flickered away from Lorraine's direct gaze. "Whatever turns you on. Just don't let Joanne know. She might get jealous." She giggled. "Are you going to the square?"

"What would I be doing over there?" asked Lorraine in her most uninterested voice and turned in the direction of the quiet coastal road outside Beachwood Village.

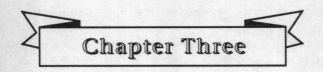

Chapter Three

F ountain Square was situated in the centre of Hobourne Park and bordered by a knee-high wall. It was graced by a large ornate fountain which had six fish-shaped jets with open mouths arching water into the air. It was a popular place for the teenagers of Beachwood to meet and gossip, to sprawl on the walls or the white wooden benches, watching boys watching girls and girls watching boys. Sometimes, if the weather was very hot, they forgot that they were dignified young people on the shores of adulthood and indulged in the most gleeful and vicious water-bomb fights. When Danny Kane took his guitar with him and played rock music, they danced on the sandy-red paving stones.

Danny sat on the low wall. He wore a Stone Roses T-shirt and was playing a track from one of their albums. Beside him, Joanne Tully sang in a low voice.

"Hey, you're good," he grinned. "How about joining my environmental rock group? I could make you a star."

"You couldn't afford me, lover boy," sighed Joanne,

staring at him from under her eye-shading fringe of brown hair.

"Don't say I never made you an offer," warned Danny.

His friend, Robbie Finlay, was lying on top of the broad wall, with his head resting on Marian Lambert's lap.

"What are you going to call this new group?" he asked.

"Dancing on Grey Ash," replied Danny.

The young people considered this in silence.

"I don't think I like it," said Marian. "It reminds me of funerals."

"More like cremations." Robbie grinned and tickled her under her chin. "You're burning me up, doll."

"I think it's cool," said Joanne. "What made you decide on it?"

"You know that story about Nero fiddling away while Rome burned around him? Well, that's the way I see things today. No one's paying any attention to what's going on in our environment. Soon we'll all be dancing on the grey ash of nuclear destruction." Danny was earnest and confident and not in the least bit confused about his ambitions. "Caro thinks it's an awful name," he admitted. "She wants me to call my group Dead Fish Don't Rap!" He sounded utterly disgusted.

Joanne shuddered in agreement. "That's gross."

Gary Crowe arrived. He was tall and well-built with an angular face and a long narrow chin. His blond hair was brushed back from his forehead and swept behind his ears. He jumped down from the wall and into the square, demanding action, fun, excitement from the teenagers who simply wanted to loll in the sun. He grabbed a can of coke from his friend, Jason Cole, and, shaking it vigorously, sprayed it over Robbie. Robbie yelled in protest and rolled over on to the ground. He wrestled half-heartedly with Gary for a few minutes until his arm was twisted behind his back and he was ordered to beg for mercy.

Jason was Gary's echo, a lanky boy with a long, skinny neck and a shock of brown curly hair that frizzed like a halo around his head. If his friend wanted action, Jason acted.

"Hey poser, give me a go!" he shouted at Danny. "I'll show you how to really play that thing." He snatched the guitar, grabbing it by the neck so that Danny's fingers slid along the strings, creating a squealing sound that made his skin crawl.

"Lay off!" He shoved Jason to one side, trying to grab back his guitar. But Jason ran towards the fountain. For one dreadful moment, Danny thought he was going to dunk his precious guitar. Jason placed his foot on the base of the fountain and slung the guitar into position.

To Danny, his guitar was a living object, made from wood that breathed, and the sounds coming from the musical instrument were pain and outrage. "You'll damage it." he shouted. "Give it back to me."

"OK, tough guy. Make me!" Jason spat into the fountain and thumped the strings a few more times. Danny, who hated physical violence and nursed his fingers as if they were rare and delicate plants, looked at the strong hands grasping his guitar. He took a deep breath. "You have two choices, Cole. Either you give me back my guitar or I fracture your face in six places."

Jason looked at him. "You and the United States Marines," he scoffed. "And even then you'd be outclassed." Danny moved nearer.

"Stop!" begged Jason. "You're terrifying me." He placed the guitar before him in mock-terror, glancing towards Gary to see if his friend appreciated his hilarious sense of humour.

But to his surprise, Gary was frowning at him.

"Give it back to him," ordered Gary.

Jason hesitated. He looked hurt, like a baby who had performed his most endearing trick and discovered that the doting adult above his playpen was not amused. Danny was equally surprised at the expression on Gary's face, as if he too had been disturbed by the ugly sounds Jason had made.

"I said, give it back to him!" repeated Gary.

"Ah here, take the damn thing. You can beat me up some other day," muttered Jason.

Danny gulped with relief and tried to look indifferent to this generous offer.

On the way home from the square, after Jason had turned off for his house, Gary walked beside Danny.

"Eh...thanks for stopping all that messing with Jason." Danny felt awkward. Thanking Gary Crowe was a new experience for him.

"Jason's a messer," said Gary, blithely ignoring the fact that when trouble spilled over, he was normally only a few paces behind it. "You wouldn't want to mind him."

"I don't. Not normally. But he'd have ruined my guitar if he'd dunked it."

"I like the guitar," said Gary. "You play it well. Are you really serious about forming that new group?"

"I might be," said Danny.

They walked on in silence for a few minutes. "Would you call around to my place on Monday with your guitar?" Gary blurted out. "I want to show you something."

Danny was about to make some excuse when he thought about Lorraine. He remembered her thin face and fair skin that blushed so easily despite her tan, her shy way of smiling. He had hoped to meet her at the square and was disappointed that she had not turned up. He knew that he wanted to see her again. But he was not sure if he wanted to call to Gary's house. Although he never wanted to admit it, he feared Gary and his sudden eruptions of temper, the way he could change from laughter to fury over an imagined insult in seconds. Sharing the same year in Beachwood Comprehensive was all they had in common and that was only because Gary had been kept back a year in primary school. Gary saw his hesitation and shrugged as if he could not care less. "It doesn't matter if you don't want to. It was just a thought. Forget it."

"No, it's OK, I'll come around."

"Great! Make it Monday evening. My mother will be out at work and I'll make us a sandwich or something."

At seven on Monday evening, Danny walked up the driveway of 4 Rockfield Heights. The hall was filled with exotic house plants, cut glass panels, paintings and an antique chair that looked as if it would collapse under the weight of a cat. A delicately-shaped gold phone rang and Gary picked it up, gesturing at Danny to go into the lounge.

Danny sat gingerly on the edge of an enormous armchair. He longed to examine the records stacked in the wooden record rack but was afraid to leave finger-prints on the album sleeves. It was that sort of house. He could not help wondering about the life cycle of a dust speck in its sterile atmosphere.

He noticed a portrait above the fireplace and recognised the imposing features of Gary's mother. She was an exotic-looking woman with high, wide cheeks, creamy skin and rust-coloured hair swept straight back from her face. She had a haughty expression as she gazed down, and weird, slanting grey eyes that seemed to follow Danny, no matter where he moved in the room, warning him to keep his hands to himself and not touch any of her precious possessions.

"Hi Danny. How's the fan-club?" A low voice drew his attention away from the portrait.

Looking around, he saw Lorraine curled up in the depths of a beanbag with a book in her hand. She was wearing floral leggings and a sloppy black T-shirt.

"Sergeant Hilliard is still trying to catch up with them." He went down on his hunkers beside her. "What are you reading?"

She showed him the cover of a book called *Hunter's Moon*.

"I read that." Danny's finger jabbed at the picture of a fox on the cover. "It was brilliant. I loved the bit about the city fox and the way he used to rob curry takeaways."

"That was good," she agreed. "But wasn't it really cruel when her mate was killed? Do you like books about animals?"

"Love them! Especially *Animal Farm*. The best bit..."

"Is this a zoo or what?" demanded Gary, who had been listening from the doorway. He slumped his shoulders and curled his arms, making gorilla movements towards his sister, snatching her book and flinging it across the room.

"Leave me alone, you big bully!" she shrieked. She tried to scramble to her feet. But he grabbed the edge of the beanbag, yanking it so hard that she tumbled over, skinny knees and elbows hitting the carpet. She looked awkward, felt awkward, blushing deeply as she stood up, pulling down her rucked T-shirt and stalking from the room.

"Stupid cow," shrugged Gary, grinning at Danny. "She's never been able to take a joke."

"Hey listen, why did you ask me over here?" said Danny. He was feeling very uncomfortable. If he tried any of that rough stuff on his sisters, they would bury him forever under their fury, and their fists.

"Come on upstairs." Gary led the way into his bedroom. Clothes and shoes covered the floor. Records and music magazines were strewn across his bed. He had his own stereo unit and television set. Both were covered in a thick layer of dust. Gary pressed his broad shoulder against a pine wardrobe, grunted and shifted it out of position. From behind it he drew out a guitar.

"Hey. That's something else!" Danny reached towards the guitar and began to strum it. "I didn't know you played."

"Neither does anyone else...except her." Gary laughed abruptly and glanced towards the wall where the faint strains of a record player could be heard from his sister's bedroom.

He took the guitar from Danny and started to play "I Still Haven't Found What I'm Looking For." He was good, his fingers moving confidently over the strings, holding the guitar as if it was an extension of his body. Danny picked up his own guitar and joined in. He began to sing in his gravelly, deep voice that always sounded as if it should belong to a much older person. They played together, forgetting everything except the rhythm of the

26

music. Danny kicked off his shoes, jumped on the bed and twisted his body into weird contortions that had his imaginary female audience on their toes and screaming.

"Eat your heart out, Bono!" he yelled when they finished. Playing music always left him on a high and his blood seemed to be humming long after the music had stopped. They played together, shouting out titles to each other and grinning with delight when they discovered that they knew all the same songs. They were both Beatle fans and ended the session with a medley of their hit songs.

"Hey, look at the time!" said Danny, amazed that two hours could pass so quickly. He put his guitar back into its case.

"Who taught you to play like that?"

Gary's head was bent. His fingers twitched but did not touch the strings. "I used to listen to my father playing." He did not look up from the guitar. "That was years ago, when I was just a kid. When I got this guitar last year, I bought a book and taught myself to play."

Danny was surprised. The Crowes had moved to Beachwood when Gary was eleven years old. He was now sixteen and Danny had never once heard him mention his father. He was about to ask what had happened to his father but the closed expression on the older boy's face told him that it would not be a good idea to pry. As if sensing his thoughts Gary said, "This is his guitar. He lives in the States." He was placing his guitar back behind the wardrobe and there was something about the savage heave he gave the wardrobe that spoke of a deep resentment.

"I'm surprised you're not playing in a group." Danny stood up to leave.

"I'm not...I'm forbidden..."Gary was having some difficulty with his words. "My mother hates the guitar," he confessed in a rush. "She's no idea that I've got this one stashed away. Don't say anything to anyone, OK?"

"Sure," Danny shrugged in agreement. "I know what it's like." His own mother kept threatening to plug her ears with cotton wool every time he started playing. Mrs Kane often worried aloud if his addiction to music was her fault because when he was a baby, she had placed a transistor radio, playing wall-to-wall music, into his cot. She declared that it was the only object that could silence his cries, a sound not unlike a wasp swarm with toothache. But even though she complained, he knew that she would never forbid him to play.

"Will you come around again?" Gary asked. The thinly-disguised plea in his voice was so unlike his normal aggressive tones that Danny found himself nodding in agreement.

When he opened the bedroom door, Lorraine was standing on the landing, facing it. Her eyes were troubled when she looked over Danny's shoulder at her brother. Then, without a word, she turned around and went back into her room, closing the door softly behind her.

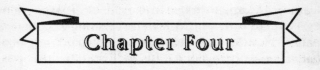

Chapter Four

Two weeks before Lorraine's birthday, she brought her dog to Beachwood Strand. Candy, released from her lead, darted off, kicking sand and wagging her tail before disappearing over the top of a sand dune. It would rain before lunch. The sky and sea merged in a dull misty grey light. Suddenly she heard snarling and the unmistakable sounds of dogs fighting. Lorraine ran up the steep slope of the sand dune, panting with fear and calling Candy's name. For a moment she could see only a whirl of legs and fur and teeth. To her horror she recognised the other dog as Beethoven, a large bulldog belonging to Stinger Muldoon. Stinger was on the other side of the dune, yelling a sharp command. He was a fisherman who lived in a little cottage in Harbour Bend. When he walked with Beethoven through Beachwood Village, young people crossed the road rather than pass the broad-backed, bow-legged, flat-nosed dog. Beethoven enjoyed his fearsome reputation. He would move his heavy head from side to side, watching everyone, his eyes sending out a signal: "Don't come too close or I'll have your bones for my second helping."

Stinger was every bit as fearsome-looking as his dog. He had a flattened nose and a head like a football, leathery-brown, wrinkled and bald. Beethoven went everywhere with him. They went fishing in Stinger's battered trawler and Beethoven would guard the catch, defying any fish to dare flick its tail once it landed in the hold. As far as Lorraine was concerned, they were the most terrifying couple in the world.

Candy was a plucky fighter but Beethoven had her ear firmly in his teeth and was not letting go. Stinger roared and the dog reluctantly loosened his grip. He looked reproachfully at his master and sidled slowly to heel. Saliva dripped from his mouth.

Lorraine flung her arms around Candy and wept into the golden fur.

"Your little dog started it, Miss," said Stinger. "She went straight for Beethoven's nose."

In her heart, Lorraine knew this was true. Candy loved to show off by squaring up to bigger dogs. But when Stinger held out a gnarled brown hand to reassure her, Lorraine screamed and ran down the sand with Candy at her heels, both of them uttering high-pitched yelps of terror. They climbed up a grassy embankment leading to the coast road and kept running until they rounded the corner of Harbour Bend where a cluster of whitewashed cottages overlooked the sea. Some of them belonged to local fishermen but two adjacent cottages had been transformed into the White Light Studio. Despite her terror, Lorraine noticed that the skylight was open. Candy had also recognised the scent of an old friend and was beginning to calm down. She barked with excitement.

"John! John!" Lorraine shrieked.

"Hey kid! What's up? Are you training for the marathon or are you just glad to see me?" John Donaldson appeared around the side entrance of his studio. He looked taken aback to see the breathless, flushed girl who was leaning over the wall, trying to catch her breath.

Lorraine immediately flung her arms around him and he swung her up in the air as if she was a bird. His eyes were like dark glossy currants in his plump face and he had a thick, bushy, black beard.

John Donaldson had been an unknown artist when he first met Zena Crowe. Soon after opening The Zany Crowe's Nest, she had called to his studio in Harbour Bend and commissioned him to paint her portrait. She wanted it to reflect a certain image and they argued with each other all the time he was painting it.

"I want it large and imposing," she told him. "I am a successful business woman and I want you to remember that fact with every brush stroke you make."

He thought she was the bossiest woman he had ever met and did exactly what he was told. He never liked the portrait but she thought it was an excellent reflection of excellence and hung it above the fireplace in her lounge. Much to his astonishment he also discovered that they had become friends during the difficult sittings and that friendship included Gary and Lorraine.

Since then, his paintings were gaining a lot of attention and exhibitions of his work had been mounted. Gary thought his paintings were a "load of old rubbish" but he often went to Mr Donaldson's studio after he had had a row with his mother. Lorraine adored him and his paintings, except for her mother's portrait. Mrs Crowe thought the haughty expression and the cold staring eyes made her look strong and decisive. But the portrait always reminded Lorraine of her mother's face whenever Jeff Crowe's name was mentioned.

The artist, who looked after Candy when Lorraine was at boarding school, tended the dog's ear and bathed her bites. Beethoven had been checked before he could really sink his teeth into flesh but Candy, asleep at Lorraine's feet, still shivered and made whimpering noises.

"Funny that you should call today," said the artist. "I was just thinking that it's your birthday soon. Time for another nosh-up at the Crowe's Nest."

Lorraine's birthdays were usually celebrated in the restaurant with her mother, Gary and John Donaldson. The staff would gather around and formally toast her with pink champagne. Lorraine always tried to convince herself that this was the perfect way to celebrate her birthday.

Her bottom lip quivered. She tried to concentrate on what the artist was saying. "How grown-up you've become. A real teenager. I suppose you're beating off the boys. It's hard to believe you'll soon be fifteen years old."

Lorraine began to cry. There was no warning. Just a great and shameful gush of tears that made her nose run and her throat tighten into a lump.

"What's this! What's this!" John Donaldson buried her in his burly arms and she sobbed against the soft flesh of his shoulder.

"Don't worry...don't worry," he kept repeating. "It's delayed reaction to shock. That's all it is."

But Lorraine, in a high, quivery voice, told him that she was a nerd and that she had no friends in Beachwood because everyone called her a swot and that she hated having her birthday in a boring old restaurant when all the other girls went to the cinema or an ice-rink or a bowling alley and ended up having a meal in McDonald's or Eddie Rocket's and that she had no figure, no matter how much time she spent doing chest exercises and that boys never asked her out and that Gary had told her that in Fountain Square they had voted her *The Girl Most Likely Never to Need a Bra.*

John Donaldson looked startled at this last piece of information. He took a handkerchief from his pocket and dried her eyes. Then he lifted a canvas from a number of stacked paintings against the wall. Without speaking, he took her hand and drew her into the brightest spot in the studio and handed a small painting to her.

"This is your birthday present. I know it's a little premature but I can't think of a better moment to give it to you."

The image on the canvas blurred but eventually she was able to focus her eyes on the painting. It showed a beach and a golden dog and a young girl staring at the waves. The colours were pastel, a blue sea merging with purple evening clouds, pink sand, the setting sun turning rockpools into flame. The wind blew the girl's dress and tossed her blonde hair so that even though she was standing still, the picture was full of energy. Lorraine studied the large, grey eyes, the curved chin, the high forehead and the slender hands. The mouth was a little too wide and the nose sloped too much to be a perfect shape. But John Donaldson had made all the features blend and belong together in the nicest way possible.

"That's not me." Her voice was full of wonder.

"That is how I see you," he said.

"But I don't look like that. You've made me so pretty." She made it sound like an accusation.

33

"What way should I have painted you?" asked the artist.

"I...I...how should I know?" She spoke defensively. "Dull and boring. Without all those colours."

"Is that how you really see yourself? Or have you listened to your brother and his inane comments so often that you're no longer willing to think for yourself?" He took the painting from her. He was so angry that his thick eyebrows seemed to bristle. But she knew that his anger was not directed at her. Then she started speaking again in the same high, rapid voice, as if she was afraid that once she stopped, she would not be able to continue.

She told him about her mother and the perfection that was demanded from her two children and how Lorraine had always bent forward to oblige her and Gary had leaned backwards to pull in the opposite direction.

Mr Donaldson looked sad. "Your mother's had a rough time, Lorraine. I know she comes across as a very successful woman. But it hasn't been easy. She's carrying a lot of memories and she won't let go of the ones that hurt the most. I wish she would." He sighed and looked wistful for a moment. "I'll have a word with her about that birthday party. Maybe it's time for a change." He pressed his thumb against her nose and she managed a watery smile. "Now, I want you to say the one word that sums up the character of the girl in this picture. Think carefully now."

After a moment, in a very low voice, Lorraine said, "Confidence."

He was smiling at her and she knew that it was the right word. She closed her eyes, feeling drained, as if she had just run a great distance.

"Can I look at my birthday present again?" Suddenly

she felt shy. Maybe she had imagined the loveliness of the girl in the painting. She stared at it once again, allowing herself a sweet glow of pleasure, allowing herself to say over and over again in a confident little whisper, "Yes, I like it. I like it very much indeed."

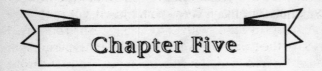

Chapter Five

Builders had started working on a kitchen extension of 4 Rockfield Heights. The sounds of lump hammers and the crash of plaster echoed through the house. But the guitar sessions continued. Gary made an effort to clear his room and it no longer looked like the aftermath of a bombing blitz. Danny had written a song called "Soul of Ivory." They experimented with the music, sang harmony and kept changing the lyrics. The story was about a magnificent elephant that had been slaughtered for his ivory tusks and ended up as a delicately-carved ivory ornament in a display cabinet in a house.

"How come I never see Lorraine in Fountain Square?" Danny asked Gary.

The older boy shrugged. "She's too stuck-up to mingle with the riffraff."

"I don't think she's a snob."

"That's because you don't know her as well as I do." He sounded contemptuous. "She's so smug. And she thinks she knows everything. I even heard her telling my mother that the Junior Cert was a breeze."

Danny clutched his throat and choked. "Don't mention the *word*!" He had promised himself that he would not think about the Junior Cert results until after the summer holidays. "You think *you've* got problems. You should try living with Caro!" His sister had borrowed his Save the Rain Forests T-shirt without his permission and given it back to him with boob-puckers in the front and the most disgusting smell of perfume from it. "And last week I found her lying in the bath in *my* 501s!" he groaned.

Gary looked sick at the idea of such atrocities being committed on his clothes. "Lorraine wouldn't dare do anything like that. I'd sort her out quickly enough."

A week later, when Danny was going to Fountain Square, he saw Lorraine in Hobourne Park with her dog. Candy immediately whimpered in excitement and jumped up on him.

"She's probably got the scent of Racky," said Danny, rubbing her fur.

"Have you got a dog?"

"Not me. It's my brother's. But I take him out a lot. Are you going to the square?"

She hesitated. "No…no…I was going to walk through the park. I don't really know the crowd."

"So you keep saying." He grinned at her. "Come on, I'll introduce you."

In Fountain Square, Joanne Tully was sitting on one of the white benches with Amanda Bell and Marian Lambert. She looked curiously at Danny and Lorraine when they jumped down from the low wall.

"You remember Lorraine Crowe?" Danny asked her.

"Of course I do. I haven't seen you around for ages,

Lorraine. How's boarding school?"

"Jolly hockey sticks and gymslips," said Amanda in a put-on posh accent.

"It's all right," said Lorraine. "When I'm away I miss Beachwood dreadfully and when I'm at home boarding school doesn't seem so bad."

"I know what you mean," said Joanne."I went away to do a summer school course last year and that's exactly how I felt."

She pushed against Amanda and made room for Lorraine on the bench. "What kind of food do you get? I nearly starved in my summer school because they kept trying to feed me raw hamburgers and mushy peas."

Lorraine shuddered in sympathy. "We get lumpy gravy and runny mashed potatoes."

"You must survive on midnight feasts then," said Marian. "That's the only reason I'd like to go to boarding school."

Lorraine's shyness was beginning to disappear. Within a short time, she was telling them all about Iona Abbey and the only midnight feast she had ever attended. A group of girls had gathered by candlelight in utter silence to devour slabs of chocolate, crisps and a huge creamy birthday cake. Everything went well until a mouse, fooled by the silence, darted out from the wall skirting. The first girl to see it uttered an ear-shattering scream. This set everyone else screaming. They leaped on chairs and beds. The terrified mouse took one look at the scene and promptly disappeared back into its hole.

But the girls had nowhere to hide. They froze like marble statues when the door opened and their form tutor appeared.

Everyone except Amanda laughed and groaned at the

punishment that had been meted out. A one-hour exercise session in the PE hall at seven every morning for two weeks.

"Play us a tune, Danny. We want to dance!" Amanda ordered him. Her voice was bossy and loud. "I love listening to you play."

He was going to refuse but he was a sucker for flattery. Joanne tried to get Lorraine to join in the dancing but she looked embarrassed and kept shaking her head. When the three girls began to dance, doing the exact same movements and laughing up a storm together, she looked as if she really wanted to be part of it all. Jason Cole gave a whoop and dragged her to her feet. He ignored her protests and twirled her around in a wild, swinging movement. Candy had been snoozing at Lorraine's feet. She opened her eyes, barked furiously, jumped up on Jason and tangled herself in Lorraine's legs. Lorraine was in the middle of a swing and, unable to recover her balance, fell heavily on the paving stones.

"Did you tie your shoelaces together again, Lorraine?" her brother shouted. "Encore! Encore!"

Some of the young people laughed. Danny decided that he never wanted to play guitar with Gary again. He offered Lorraine a rather grubby tissue. She brushed him aside and told him in a very prissy voice that it didn't matter. Her eyes were swimming with tears of pain and she looked miserably embarrassed, conscious that everyone was watching her. The knee of one of her leggings had ripped. Flayed skin and Lycra mingled in a blood-soaked mess.

Joanne linked her arm and made her sit down on the bench. She knelt in front of Lorraine's knee and picked out pieces of gravel. Then she soaked her handkerchief in the fountain and tried to clean the blood stains. When the knee continued to pump blood, Joanne told her friends that she was bringing Lorraine home to disinfect and bandage the wound.

"But it's only a scratch!" Amanda sounded impatient. "It'll be all right in a minute."

"No, it won't," said Joanne. "It's very deep." She sounded so protective that Amanda glowered, not looking at all pleased with the development of this new friendship. After the two girls left, she said loudly that she didn't understand why such a fuss was being made over a little graze and it was quite obvious that Lorraine Crowe was deliberately putting on that limp.

"How's Lorraine's knee?" Danny asked Gary the following afternoon.

"Fine. It was nothing much. Dr Darcy gave her an anti-tetanus injection for it."

"Then it must have been bad."

"She makes a fuss about nothing. It didn't stop her going down to the beach afterwards with Joanne Tully." Gary dismissed his sister's injury.

"I don't want to play guitar today." Danny cleared his throat.

"Neither do I," agreed Gary. "Not with that racket going on." In the kitchen underneath, the rhythmic sound of a lump hammer hitting concrete pounded through Danny's head.

"They're knocking down the kitchen wall. I'll go nuts if I don't get out of this place." Gary put the guitar back behind the wardrobe.

"Listen, I'm very tied up—" Danny began to speak but Gary interrupted him.

"I've been thinking. If you're interested in a rhythm

guitarist when you get that group going, I'd like to have a go."

Danny said nothing. He enjoyed playing music with Gary but he still had not changed his opinion of him. Gary was too quick-tempered, too moody. Playing together was sure to bring out tensions in both of them and he knew he would not be able to cope with Gary's bossiness.

"I haven't made any decision about the group yet. What about your mother? I thought you said she'd freak if she knew you had a guitar."

"I'm going to tell her." Gary ran his fingers nervously through his hair. He opened a dressing table drawer and began to rummage through some papers. From the bottom of the pile, he took out a photograph. It showed a man with shoulder-length hair tied in a ponytail and a thin, craggy face. He wore a muscle T-shirt and tight jeans. His body was arched backwards and his guitar thrust forward. He reminded Danny of the older pop stars that he saw on television with lived-in faces and loads of memories. They normally sent his father into a state of pure nostalgia. The scrawled autograph underneath read *Caley Jones*.

Danny looked enquiringly at Gary.

"Who's he?"

"My father."

"Your father? How's he got a name like Caley Jones then?"

"It's a stage name. His real name is Jeff. He's going to be a big star some day."

Gary turned the photograph over. "Play music, son!" was scrawled across the back.

"That's what I've been doing since you came over

here, Danny. It's meant a lot to me. Thanks." Gary looked at Danny then hurriedly averted his eyes in case Danny would think he was going soft. "I'm sick keeping secrets. I want to play music in a group, just like he did. He left home because my mother wouldn't let him play his guitar. She's not going to do the same to me!"

Carefully, he put the photograph back in place and closed the drawer. His voice was filled with determination when he repeated: "She's not going to do the same to me!"

Chapter Six

I t was wonderful to have a friend like Joanne. Lorraine had forgotten that she was so nice. They talked about many different things, compared favourite television programmes, records and books. Lorraine thought *Jane Eyre* was the best book she had ever read. Joanne opted for *Flowers in the Attic* and offered to lend it to her. Lorraine confessed that she was dreadfully shy and self-conscious and that she always thought other people were laughing at her behind her back. Joanne looked amazed and said, "But why should anyone laugh at you?" Lorraine discovered that she had no easy answer. But Joanne understood the feeling of being self-conscious and admitted that she sometimes felt like that, especially just before her period when she believed that she had been born with the word "nerd" branded on her forehead.

On Sunday afternoon, they brought Candy to Hobourne Park for a run. The girls sat on a bench, watching Candy darting between the trees until she barked excitedly and darted off to greet another dog.

"Oh, I hope she doesn't get into a fight again!" Lorraine called her sharply to heel. But Candy had stopped and, tail held high, was sniffing and nuzzling an elegant, auburn-coated setter. The setter patiently allowed this inspection. He was a good-natured dog and Candy felt no inclination to bite his nose. Soon their tails were wagging cheerfully. They raced across the grass, yapping excitedly.

"Hey, Racky!" Danny Kane whistled sharply. The dog paid no attention to him. Joanne nudged Lorraine sharply in the ribs as he strolled over.

"Am I red?" she hissed, putting her hands over her cheeks. "Oh no! I'm flaming!"

"No, you're not. You look really cool," whispered Lorraine. The two girls turned and stared blankly at Danny.

"I thought I recognised your dog, Lorraine. Hi Joanne. You're just the person I've been looking for."

"Jonathan will go spare if he hears you calling his dog Racky," said Joanne.

"Come off it. You don't expect me to go around shouting his real name?"

"But he won't answer to anything else," said Joanne. She cupped her hands around her mouth. "Rachmaninov. Here Rachmaninov."

Immediately the setter dashed out from the trees and came towards them. He put his paws on Joanne's knees and gave her face a slurping lick.

"Ugh!" shrieked Joanne.

"Serves you right for using that stupid name," snorted Danny.

Candy barked commandingly and Rachmaninov raced back to her. Danny told Lorraine that his older brother,

Jonathan, was mad about classical music and had insisted on calling his dog after the Russian composer and pianist. He had then trained Rachmaninov not to answer to the various nicknames used by his family, a habit which he found quite insulting and demeaning to the memory of a great man.

"Talking about music of a different sort," said Danny, looking at Joanne. "I'm keen to get the new group going. Would you like to be the female singer?"

Joanne sighed and placed her index finger thoughtfully on her cheek. "I don't know, Danny. I'm not sure if it's the career break I'm looking for."

"I'd hate to interfere with your career prospects," said Danny. "If you're not interested, I was thinking of asking Marian Lambert."

"She'll only sound good if you put a bucket over her head first," declared Joanne, scornfully. "I'll do it."

"Great. We'll call a meeting soon. I'd better go. I've to see Robbie about something. See you, Lorraine."

He stood up and whistled. The setter ignored him.

"Racky!" ordered Danny, in his firmest voice.

"I told you!" Joanne smirked.

"Rachmaninov! You stupid thick! Come here!" roared Danny. The red setter bounded happily towards him.

"I don't believe it. I don't believe it. I'm going to be a singer." Joanne was pink with excitement. She could talk about nothing else all the way home. She confided in Lorraine that she had fancied Danny for ages.

"Does he fancy you?" asked Lorraine.

"We always dance together at the discos and we hang out in school, in the canteen and walking home, all that sort of stuff. But he's always got his head up in the clouds composing this off-the-wall stuff about radioactive fish and polluted politicians." She grinned. "It's dreadful stuff but I adore him anyway."

Now that she had confessed her secret to Lorraine she could not stop talking about Danny. "He's never actually said anything about fancying me. But sometimes he looks at me and it's all sort of wobbly and kind of exciting and oh...you know how it is?"

Lorraine nodded, trying to look as if she felt "all sort of wobbly" seven nights a week. By the time they reached home, she had heard about the time the Beachwood Comprehensive third years went on their school trip to France and how Joanne and Danny stood together on the deck of the ferry with the moon shining like a ripe orange overhead. It would have sounded quite nauseating if anyone other than Joanne had been telling the story. Lorraine heard about the end-of-term celebrations when the Junior Certificate examination had finished and the pupils dived off Shale Head, fully clothed. In the water, they had danced in wild circles, singing at the top of their voices. Danny had lifted Joanne up on his shoulders and staggered up and down Beachwood Strand until they both collapsed with laughter into the sand dunes.

Lorraine figured that it would be difficult for any boy not to fancy Joanne. She had such a friendly manner and she was so pretty with her tangled long fringe and husky voice. Lorraine envied her. But it was a feeling without malice. She was happy that Joanne was happy.

She wanted nothing more than that their friendship would grow and they would confide lots of secrets to each other.

The birthday celebration was on. Lorraine could not believe so much had happened in a week. Joanne had been delighted to accept her birthday invitation to go to the cinema. Marian shrieked with pleasure when told they were going to see *Wayne's World*. Amanda accepted with a patronising smile that suggested she was willing to give some of her busy time to Lorraine as a special favour. Mrs Crowe had suggested that she bring the girls for a meal in The Zany Crowe's Nest afterwards. But Lorraine said she would prefer the Pizza Palace. Mrs Crowe sniffed disdainfully. She considered the Pizza Palace to be a cheap and very tacky place compared to The Zany Crowe's Nest. Lorraine suspected that John Donaldson had been talking to her mother because, apart from saying that she hoped Lorraine was not going to get hooked on junk food, she gave her permission.

The girls walked to the World United Cinemas complex, which everyone in Beachwood called The WUC. When they arrived, the foyer was crowded. Lorraine bought sweets and massive buckets of popcorn. Joanne's mother had given her money to buy soft drinks for everyone. Arms laden, they joined the queue.

A small, dark-haired girl was standing on her toes at the cash point, insisting that she was eighteen.

"Look at Caro Kane trying to get into an over 18 film," hissed Amanda. "Remember all the hassle she caused over The Flame of the Passion."

"We're aflame—for Danny Kane!" Joanne chanted softly. The girls fell against each other with laughter.

Another girl joined in the "Of course I'm eighteen" argument. "That's Jennifer Hilliard," grinned Joanne. "I'd know her voice anywhere. She's only fourteen. If her father could see her now he'd have a fit."

The woman behind the cash point was polite but firm. The girls were not allowed to see the film and she would call the manager if they wanted to make their point of view known. Caro wondered why such acts of discrimination were always being practised upon the youth of Ireland. The cashier had heard it all before and said: "Next please" in an extremely bored voice. When the queue made growling noises of impatience, the girls shrugged their shoulders and admitted defeat.

"Oh, tough luck, Caro," breathed Amanda when the small girl walked past.

Caro grinned and ruefully arched a pair of thick, dark eyebrows. Lorraine thought she looked very like Danny. The same twitch to her lips before she smiled and that funny way of tilting her head when she was looking at someone. "Ah well, it was worth a try. We'll have to settle for *Batman Returns* instead."

"Do you know Lorraine Crowe?" asked Joanne. "It's her birthday today."

Caro was staring at Lorraine with open curiosity. "Isn't it your house that Danny goes to all the time?"

Joanne stiffened. Amanda smirked. Marian began to hum. Lorraine blushed. She felt the colour tingling all the way down to her toes. Gary had warned her repeatedly not to tell anyone about the guitar sessions. "No, he doesn't...not really..."

"What do you mean, 'not really?'" Amanda interrupted. "I've seen him going into your place."

"You never told..." Joanne stopped talking and placed her fingers over her lips.

"I didn't want to upset you." Amanda oozed sympathy over her.

"Hey Caro. We'd better join the *Batman* queue," Jennifer nudged her sharply.

"I've got to go. See you around." Caro looked relieved as she darted away, leaving an uneasy silence behind her.

48

The girls had reached the top of the queue. Lorraine busied herself with tickets and money, trying to ignore the whispering voices behind her.

By the time the film was half over, Joanne had not laughed once. When she went into the *Ladies*, Lorraine followed her. She stood in front of the mirror and watched Joanne washing her hands. "I'm not the reason why Danny Kane comes to my house."

Joanne carefully soaped her palms. "It's no skin off my nose what Danny Kane does."

"It's to see Gary, that's what it's about."

"He was never friends with your brother. Why should he start now?" She dragged the hand towel roughly along its roll and dried her hands. Then she fluffed her fringe in the mirror and avoided looking at Lorraine.

Lorraine hesitated. She wanted so much to hold on to this friendship.

"Can you keep a secret?" she asked.

Joanne frowned and stared back at her. "If you're going to tell me that you're going out with Danny, that will be common knowledge after tonight."

"Gary and Danny, they play guitar together."

"I don't believe you. I've never even heard Gary talk about a guitar let alone play one."

"It's my father's guitar." Lorraine looked blank-faced at her friend. She found it impossible to talk about her father, even to Joanne. "Gary's been playing it for about a year. I promised him I'd keep it a secret. My mother doesn't know he has it. She can't bear anything belonging to my father in the house."

Joanne grabbed Lorraine's hands. "Oh don't, Lorraine. You look as if you're going to cry. I'm sorry for upsetting you."

"But you don't believe me!"

"I do. I do. Honest!"

"Promise you won't say a word."

"I won't. I promise. Not that it matters what Danny does. I've no claim on…"

"Come on, dope. We'll miss the film." Lorraine grabbed her arm and dragged her out of the *Ladies*.

After they were seated, Joanne leaned over. "Is Gary going to be part of Danny's group?" She sounded alarmed.

"I doubt it. He's too afraid of my mother."

"I'm glad that he's afraid of someone. I used to hate the way he treated you."

"Did you really?"

"Yes! Remember when he had to stay back a year and he came into our class? He was mad jealous of you because you were so brainy. We used to think he was a jerk."

Lorraine squeezed her hand. She felt warm and content sitting in the dark cinema, listening to her friend, Joanne, laughing louder than anyone else for the rest of the film.

Chapter Seven

"The answer is no!" Danny looked embarrassed but his voice was firm.

"Why not?" demanded Gary.

Danny placed his guitar carefully across his knee, as if to shield himself from Gary's incredulous expression. "It's nothing personal. I think you're a good guitarist. But you should consider forming your own group."

"You're afraid I'll outclass you, is that it?"

"Don't be stupid!" snapped Danny. His carefully rehearsed excuses were slipping away. Apart from talking to Joanne about becoming the female singer and thinking about asking Gerry Hilliard (he used to play keyboard with The Flame of the Passion) if he would like to join the group, Danny had done nothing else about forming Dancing on Grey Ash. His reason was simple. Gary was driving him mad. He believed that he should be an essential part of the new group. He thought the name Dancing on Grey Ash was too serious. It would not grab the public imagination and should be changed to something more cool. He was horrified at the idea of Joanne joining. All that tangled hair and big lips. Too Tina Turnerish. They needed a Sinead O'Connor. Doe eyes and no hair. Gary was no longer interested in playing rhythm. He wanted to sing and play lead guitar. Danny would be better on rhythm and his voice was too gravelly to be sexy. But the idea of focusing on the environment really got to him. No way, man.

The environment was a bore, off the teenage agenda. What kid was going to listen to songs about elephant souls and torched rain forests? Why not call themselves Voodoo Boy Vibes and concentrate on teenage rebellion "I Don't Like Mondays" sort of stuff?

This kind of talk was causing Danny sleepless nights. He could see his authority being eroded with every day that Gary believed he was part of Dancing on Grey Ash. Finally he blurted out his feelings. This band was Danny's baby. He was going to be its lead guitarist. And he wanted to pick a bass instead of a rhythm guitarist.

Gary's bottom lip puckered as if it had been stung by a wasp. His eyes narrowed. There was nothing pleading about him now. When Danny tried to explain why the line-up could not hold an extra guitarist, Gary ignored him. He switched on his compact player and the house rocked to the techno sound of The KLF. It boomed out above the lump hammers and blow torches and clattering boots of the builders who were still working on the kitchen extension.

"Shut it off," shouted Danny. "We need to talk about this."

Gary picked up his guitar and began to play along with the music.

"Stuff you! I'm going!" Danny reached for his denim

jacket.

Neither boy heard the bedroom door open. The explosive sound of The KLF slithered to a halt when Mrs Crowe jerked the plug of the stereo from the wall socket.

"Just what do you think you're doing?" she demanded.

Gary's fingers froze on the guitar strings. The twanging sound of the notes seemed to vibrate through the room. "I didn't expect you home so early," he gasped.

"Obviously not!" Mrs Crowe stared at the guitar in his hands as if it was a ghost. "Where did you get that instrument?" she gasped.

Her son looked astonished, as if he had just noticed the guitar for the first time. "It belongs to him." He nodded towards Danny.

"Don't lie to me!" She stood in front of her son. Danny noticed that her hands were trembling and she clenched them into fists.

Gary tried to grin defiantly and failed. "My father gave it to me." His words were hardly audible.

"What did you just say?" demanded Mrs Crowe.

Gary's fingers hovered over the strings.

"He gave it to me. He's not like you. He wants me to play music!"

"Give it to me." Zena Crowe spoke very quietly. "Hand it over to me, immediately."

"No! I won't." The guitar seemed moulded to his body. "I want to play it. Can't you just listen to me? I'm good. I'm really good."

"No! I don't want to hear you!" She put her hands over her ears.

Gary ran his fingers along the strings. The sound was thumping and discordant. He stopped, took a deep breath and began again. His mother winced.

Gary hit the side of the guitar in frustration then wildly attacked the strings.

"How dare you defy me," Mrs Crowe shrieked.

Gary immediately stopped playing.

"I'm not putting up with this behaviour. You're so selfish! Irresponsible and self-centred just like...like..."

"Just like my father," said Gary. His face was red, raw with anger.

"Give me that guitar at once!" demanded Mrs Crowe.

For a moment mother and son stared at each other. Then Gary wilted beneath her anger and handed over the guitar.

She held it as if it was ready to self-destruct.

"What are you going to do with it?" Gary was breathing in a heavy, wheezy way.

"I'm not having his guitar in this house. That's all you need to know." She left the room, slamming the door behind her.

Danny bit hard on his lip. He had been terrified of the tall woman with the hard commanding eyes. He wanted to slide silently away without attracting any attention. But the sight of Gary slumped on the edge of his bed made him stay.

"That was awful!" He touched the older youth's shoulder. "Really rough stuff."

Gary shrugged away from him. "Lay off, Kane, and just mind your own business. You're probably delighted that I won't be able to join your crummy band." He glared at Danny, a gaze that spelled trouble in the future. "You're nothing but a poser. I'd have played you off the stage and that's what you were afraid of."

"Suit yourself!" snapped Danny, his sympathy disappearing. "Just because your mother gives you a hard time doesn't mean you have to take it out on me."

In an instant he was flattened against the wall. Gary's hand twisted the hard fabric on the neck of his jacket, tightening it in a jerking vicious movement. Danny struggled, gasped with shock when he felt the pressure around his neck. He pushed Gary away.

"Get your hands off me, you jerk! You're right. I'm glad you're not in my group. You're nothing but trouble!"

He was on the landing before he remembered his guitar. In the same instant that he tried to return to the bedroom, he heard the lock turn.

"Give me back my guitar, Crowe!" he shouted, hitting the wood with his fist. Silence greeted his demand. "I want it back," he shouted.

"Get out of my house immediately!" said Mrs Crowe. She stood at the top of the stairs and eyed Danny as if he had just crawled out from underneath a very flat stone. Any thought of returning to claim his guitar vanished. Danny ducked his head and kept running, almost hitting the huge rubbish skip that had been placed in the driveway to take away the rubble from the kitchen extension.

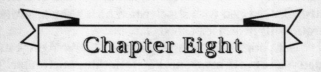

Chapter Eight

T he previous week, Mrs Crowe had told Lorraine that trying to pin Larry the builder down to a date when work would be finished on the extension was more difficult than hand-catching fish in a barrel of oil. He had promised that not even a speck of cement would be left lying around before the start of his holidays in August. But for the next two weeks, the Crowe family would have to cope with their half-completed kitchen while Larry lay beneath the Spanish sun and drank Sangria.

"There's only a few small things to finish." He tried to placate Mrs Crowe. "I'll have them done for you the day I get back."

"Small things! I've no back wall to my kitchen," cried Mrs Crowe. "As well as that rubbish skip monstrosity blocking my driveway."

"The wall will be finished by tomorrow evening before we leave. And you have the electricity on again. As well as the water. You'll be as snug as a bug in a rug until I get back." Larry made their kitchen extension with its flapping sheets of canvas, clouds of dust and gaping holes sound like paradise.

Lorraine had just arrived back from the beach. She thought that her mother's strained expression and swollen red-rimmed eyes were due to the trouble she was having with Larry.

"Did Larry make you cry?" Lorraine asked after the builder left.

Mrs Crowe shook her head. She said that she had come home early from the restaurant to see how the work on the kitchen extension was going and the dust raised by the workmen seemed to have given her an eye infection. When Gary banged open the kitchen door and raided the fridge, Lorraine knew immediately that there had been a row between them. His mother spoke to the back of his head, informing him that he would be working full-time with her for the rest of the school holidays.

"Starting tomorrow," she snapped. "You can assist Jack in the kitchen."

"You'll have to drag me there," he retorted.

"If I have to, I will," promised Mrs Crowe.

The atmosphere in the house was so creepy that Lorraine went to her room. After her mother left for the restaurant, Lorraine heard a muffled, thudding sound coming from Gary's room.

"Gary! Are you all right?"

"Get lost!" he shouted back. His voice was husky.

"I'm only trying to help."

"You can help by getting out of my hair," he retorted. "What would you know about anything? You always get your own way in this house."

"That's not true!"

Gary, she decided, was his own worst enemy. It was impossible to feel sorry for him. He would be out of the house every day and she would have it all to herself. She could bring her friends in and not worry that her brother would try and make her look stupid.

Next morning, Mrs Crowe's eye infection had disappeared. She outlined the house rules to Lorraine. Lorraine could bring only two girl friends into the house and no boys. Everyone must be out of the house by eight at night. She wrote out a list of chores that Lorraine had to do and gave her a Sunday afternoon shift in the restaurant for the remainder of the summer holidays. It was time she began to earn some money, instead of expecting her mother to pay for everything, particularly if she was going to start buying things like eighteen-hole Docs.

"Eight holes." Lorraine corrected her mother. "I'm not a punk!" She was going into Dublin city with Joanne that afternoon to buy them. Joanne had told her that there was a place at the back of the Ilac Centre that had a brilliant selection of Doc Martens.

The city was crowded with shoppers wearing shorts and sandals. Children licked ice creams and bathed their feet in the Anna Livia water monument in O'Connell Street. The two girls sampled perfume in The Body Shop. Joanne bought a stripy bodysuit and a pair of hot pants in A Wear. Then they fought their way through the crowds in McDonald's.

"My mother said that civilisation took a step backwards the day they introduced plastic forks," said Lorraine, chewing blissfully on a Big Mac.

Two young men sat at their table and started talking to them. They were very old, about nineteen at least, and

Lorraine was too embarrassed to know what to say to them. They told the girls they were film stars on location, making a film in the Temple Bar area. Tom Cruise was a personal friend, they said, and they partied regularly with Madonna.

They had really fake American accents and kept laughing at each other's jokes. Joanne told them she was a singer on the edge of a major career break.

"So, where do you gig?" asked one, forgetting his accent.

"Next week it's the Point Depot," she replied, straight-faced.

"Pull the other one!" said the man called Hunk. "What about your friend? What's her game?"

"She's a Brain!" said Joanne, proudly. "She is an intellectual genius. The female Einstein."

"Oh, get lost!" spluttered Lorraine, almost choking on her Big Mac.

The men wanted their telephone numbers.

"Sorry," said Joanne. "No dice."

"Have you got a boyfriend or what?" asked Hunk.

"I have," she replied.

"What about you?" he turned to Lorraine. "You hitched up to anyone?"

"Em...well...actually—"

"Actually, *Chunk*, she's too busy being a genius to be impressed by two Southside posers!" said Joanne and swept Lorraine down the stairs and out into O'Connell Street. They laughed all the way to the bus stop.

"There was a young lad looking for you," said Brendan, the plasterer, on their return. He was putting the final touches to the back wall. "He called around a few times. Said his name was Danny something or other."

"Danny Kane?" said Joanne. She placed her parcels on the floor and did not look at Lorraine.

"It must have been Gary he wanted," Lorraine insisted.

"No, it was you all right." He winked at Joanne. "Is he her boyfriend? He seemed awfully keen to see her."

"I wouldn't know," muttered Joanne.

"He is not!" exclaimed Lorraine. She had no reason to feel guilty yet she knew she was blushing, furiously.

Next day, she met Danny in Fountain Square. "I want to talk to you about something," he said and drew her away from the crowd. "I was looking for you yesterday. I wanted to know if you could help me."

"What's wrong?"

"It's that meat-loaf brother of yours. He's got my guitar. But whenever I manage to track him down, he keeps denying it. He says he hasn't seen it anywhere." Danny shrugged in exasperation. "How can he say that? I left it in his bedroom."

"Don't mind him. He's been in awful humour over some row he had with my mother."

"I know. I was there." Briefly, he told her what had happened.

She nodded, without surprise. "I knew he'd be discovered sooner or later. I'm sure your guitar is still where you left it. Gary's just being difficult. I'll find it when I go home and give you a ring."

He put his hands on her shoulders. "How did someone as nice as you manage to get lumbered with a brother like that?"

"He's not so bad," she replied. She felt uneasy, wriggling away from him when Joanne strolled up.

"Promise you won't forget to ring me," Danny asked, anxiously.

"I promise," she replied in a low voice and glanced quickly around at Joanne.

"It's too hot to hang around the square. We're going down to the beach." Joanne walked past. She sounded very cool and aloof.

Lorraine hurried after her. "What's the matter, Joanne?"

Her friend stopped and stared keenly at her. "It's like this, Lorraine, I've told you a lot of stuff. Stuff about Danny that I haven't told anyone else. I don't want to make a fool of myself. If there's anything I should know...!"

"Don't be daft!" Lorraine linked her arm. "There's nothing to tell. Nothing at all."

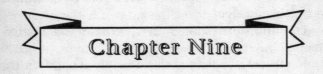

Chapter Nine

"It's for you, Danny. It's your girl for-end," screamed Caro.

She rolled her eyes and pretended to faint with excitement. He snatched the phone from her and tried to gag her mouth with his other hand.

"Hi Danny. It's Lorraine Crowe."

Danny nudged his sister away from the phone where she kept mouthing the word "girl for-end" at him. Lorraine, unaware of the pantomime at the other end of the line, continued speaking. "I've searched everywhere for the guitar but I can't find it anywhere."

"But it has to be there. What's he done with it? I'm going over to your place to look for myself." He slammed down the phone before she could reply.

The large rubbish skip blocked the driveway. Danny was dodging around it when Lorraine opened the door.

"You look like you're about to have a heart attack," she said. "I'll make you a mug of coffee before you start taking this place apart."

He followed her into the kitchen. It smelled of dried plaster and there was a gritty, dusty feeling in the air. The extension had still not been completed but the old part of the kitchen was functional. Lorraine made coffee and opened a packet of chocolate ring biscuits. Danny carried the tray into the lounge. The portrait of Zena Crowe stared down upon them, eyeing them sternly. It made Danny even more aware that they were alone in the house. The thought made him uneasy and excited at the same time.

"Will your mother ever give Gary back his father's guitar?" he asked.

Lorraine shook her head. "It's a really tense subject. Gary gets letters from his father. He's even been to America to see him. But she never talks about it when Gary comes home and she pretends not to notice the letters. Gary looks very like his father."

"I know."

"How do you know that?" She seemed surprised.

"Gary showed me a photograph of him. Do you have one?"

Vehemently, she shook her head. "I think it's hard for her...Gary seems to remind her of all that went wrong. That's why he hid the guitar. He knew she'd never allow it in the house."

Danny noticed how she said "his father" as if the words had no place in her life. "What about you? Do you see your father?"

"I don't want to. I've no interest in him." She cradled the coffee mug in her hands and stared into it, deliberately changing the subject. "Joanne's really excited about Dancing on Grey Ash."

"You and Joanne have become very close." Danny

tilted his head quizzingly at her.

"She's lovely," replied Lorraine and smiled, warmly.

"She's a smashing singer."

"Do you like her?" Lorraine asked. She placed her coffee mug carefully back on the tray.

"I sure do. She's great fun."

"I mean...as in...fancy her?" When she bent her head, her hair fell across her face, hiding her cheeks.

"Gosh, no! She'd howl if she heard you saying that." Danny was amazed at her question. He had been friends with Joanne since they were children. They talked about everything together. Next to Robbie, she was his best mate. "Whatever made you ask that?"

"Just wondered," replied Lorraine and picked up the tray. For some reason, neither of them could think of anything to say.

"We'd better start searching for my guitar." He cleared his throat, nervously.

"I can't figure where it is," she said, leading the way into the hall. "We'll check everything, even the most stupid places. If it's here, we're sure to find it."

An hour later, they were on the verge of admitting defeat. Even the attic had been tried, the two of them stumbling over bundles of comics, old school books and black refusacks of clothes.

The last room they entered was Lorraine's. It was beautifully furnished with mirrored built-in wardrobes, shelves laden with cute fluffy animals and hanging plants. A porcelain doll with frilly petticoats was arranged decoratively on a white wicker chair. Bowls of pot pourri sweetened the air.

"This is some pad compared to my sister's bedroom," said Danny, whistling through his teeth. "My mother says a body could get lost in there and never find the way to the door again."

Caro used her bedroom as a tortoise uses its shell, drawing into its shelter when she was annoyed or troubled, living her private life amidst its jumble of books and clothes, scribbling in her diary, lolling on the bed with her friends, gossiping, giggling and exchanging secrets. It was difficult to imagine Lorraine ever flinging a pair of jeans over her bed. Or sitting in her show house bedroom for hours with her friends. She seemed to read his thoughts.

"I never feel that it's really my own room," she confessed. "My mother had it decorated for me when I was away at school. She likes things to be just right. I'd love to paint the ceiling red and pin posters of Bon Jovi on the wall instead of that junk." She pointed to a row of framed certificates. They had been awarded for speech and drama, ballet, swimming and any other activity which proved that Lorraine Crowe had been involved in the pursuit of excellence. "She says that life is too short to be wasted on anything other than excellence."

"My mother says it's too short to skin peppers and sweep under mats," said Danny.

"I don't think they'd get on," admitted Lorraine. For a moment they forgot about the guitar and the two of them laughed together in the most witless fashion.

"Did your mother choose this?" Danny noticed the painting on the wall.

"No. That belongs entirely to me."

"It's brilliant," he said.

"John Donaldson did it."

"Not the same guy who did that awful...I mean that awesome painting downstairs?"

"That's him."

"This is much better. It's exactly like you. Everything's right."

He could not take his eyes off it. Lorraine looked very pleased. She told him about the day she had first seen the painting, when she had fled in terror from Stinger Muldoon.

"Stinger's all right," said Danny. "My brother Jonathan says he has a brilliant collection of classical albums. He goes over to his place in Harbour Bend to hear them."

"You're having me on!" The thought of Stinger and Danny's yuppy brother with his fancy clothes and carefully groomed appearance sitting listening to classical music made Lorraine laugh even louder.

"They called their dogs after their favourite composers."

"I know." She hiccupped and wiped her eyes. "How's Rachmaninov?"

"As disobedient as ever. We should take our dogs for a walk some day."

Lorraine did not reply. From the window of her room, they could see the hazy glow of the porch lantern. It outlined the garden shrubs and the huge rubbish skip straddling the driveway like a monstrous toad. With a swishing sound, she drew the curtains. The bedside lamp cast a rosy glow over the room, adding to the cosy and intimate atmosphere.

"We'd better go downstairs," she said.

Danny did not move. He wondered if she could feel his heart thudding when he reached forward and put his arms around her. His lips brushed her cheek and, with the palm of one hand, he gently turned her face towards him. He had never seen her eyes up close, a deep, cloudy-grey colour, warm eyes that were staring at him just as keenly as he was staring at her. They kissed, a brief touch of lips before she pulled abruptly away.

"Don't do that!" she said. Her expression was troubled as if some image had flashed into her mind.

Immediately he moved away from her. He did not know what to do with his hands and plunged them into the pockets of his jeans.

"You'd better go. There'll be trouble if my mother finds out you've been in the house." She could have been speaking to a stranger. He felt as if he had been dashed with a bucket of cold water.

"I'm sorry. I thought...I'm sorry."

"You thought wrong, Danny," she said. "I'm not interested in you. Not like that."

He nodded his head. "I'll remember."

She tried to ease their embarrassment. "I'm really sorry about the guitar. But you can see for yourself. It's not here."

His face darkened. The thought that he might never get his guitar back filled him with dread. "Tell your brother that I'll take him apart if he doesn't return it."

"I'll talk to Gary tomorrow. But don't call around to the house again. I don't want people to get the wrong idea about us."

"Who cares what people think?" he said.

"I do," she replied and her voice was very firm as she opened the front door and waited for him to leave. He did not notice Amanda Bell at her bedroom window or see her thoughtful smile as she pulled across her curtains. In bed, he thumped his pillow, shook it vigorously, determined to shake Lorraine Crowe out of his mind. Then he fell asleep and dreamt about nothing else for the rest of the night.

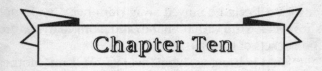

Chapter Ten

S unday was a busy day at The Zany Crowe's Nest.
   There was a special Sunday lunch for families.
Tourists, visiting Beachwood Strand, added to the
numbers. Lorraine often helped out in the restaurant
when it was short-staffed, so her mother put her in
charge of three tables. She was too busy to think about
anything except who had ordered what and how she
could console a heart-broken, three-year-old boy who
burst into tears when he discovered that the neatly-
rolled, snowy-white table napkin with the deep pink
border was something he had to tuck under his chin and
was not, as he had thought, a strawberry ripple ice cream.

Fiona, one of the waitresses, gave her a sympathetic
smile. "Get him an ice cream from the kitchen. Otherwise
he'll drive the customers out the door."

Temper-tantrums flared easily in the steaming, hissing,
humming kitchen of The Zany Crowe's Nest. Jack was
the head chef, king of the kitchen, the only member of
staff who dared address his boss as "Zany." Gary's job was

to assist him. He was chopping stir-fry vegetables, slowly and clumsily. Jack had been bossing him since the shift started and he looked belligerently at his sister.

"What was Danny Kane doing in our house last night?" he demanded.

Lorraine stopped in her tracks, horrified. "Who told you that?"

"Everyone knows. It's all over the square."

The heat of the kitchen seemed to rise sharply. Lorraine touched her cheeks. "If you want to know, we were searching for Danny's guitar. He says you have it."

"That's a lie!" Gary presented a picture of hurt innocence. "He was just using that as an excuse because he knew you'd be on your own in the house. Even if I had it, why would I *hide* his guitar in *your* bedroom?"

"What do you mean? Who says he was in my bedroom?"

"You were seen, both of you. Talk about being indiscreet. I wonder what she'd say if she knew." He nodded towards his mother, who was speaking to Jack. "Little Miss Goody-Two-Shoes breaking the number one rule."

"We weren't doing anything wrong. We'd tried everywhere else!"

"For a non-existent guitar! Pull the other one."

"You're a thief, Gary Crowe!" Lorraine could feel her temper flaring. This time, he was not going to intimidate her.

"And you're a tart, Lorraine Crowe," he retorted. He sliced a carrot and the knife banged loudly on the chopping board. Before Gary had time to duck, Lorraine had gripped the slippery tail of a large salmon that was waiting on the table to be grilled. She swung wildly, smacking Gary on his face with it. He yelled and tried to grab the fish. When it slipped between their hands, he kicked it across the floor.

"What on earth is going on here?" their mother demanded. She strode towards them, then wildly clawed the air when her foot touched the salmon.

It slithered like a skateboard beneath her and she landed on the kitchen floor. The crash rattled the saucepans and the cutlery danced with shock. Jack rushed to pick her up. He too lost his balance and fell on top of her. Gary ran from the kitchen and collided with Fiona, who was carrying a tray. Dishes shot into the air and turned upside down. Diners stared, fascinated, as the law of gravity prevailed and a dish of mixed salad landed on a man's head. With coleslaw oozing from his hair, he ran around The Zany Crowe's Nest, roaring about compensation and solicitors and revenge. At another table, a sole on the bone nestled in a woman's lap. It stared up at her from one glassy eye. The woman screamed and spilled a glass of white wine over it. Roderick, the wine waiter, dashed from the kitchen carrying a basin of hot water and knelt before her. He removed the sole on the bone from her skirt and dabbed at her knees with a wet, white napkin. The woman screamed again and slapped his face.

Jack fluttered his hands and nervously eyed his boss. He kept repeating, "You're all right now, Zany…you're all right now, Zany," in a voice that sounded as if he had absolutely no hope of being believed.

Fiona opened the kitchen door and peeped out. "Mrs Crowe, the customers are rioting. You'd better go out and talk to them."

When Zena Crowe emerged from behind the door

marked *Private*, a brilliant smile stretched her lips. No one dared tell her that the seat of her dress was covered in an enormous grease stain.

She made soothing noises and ordered bottles of wine (compliments of the restaurant) to be sent to the tables of her ruffled customers. Within a few minutes, peace had been restored and a contented three-year-old was tucking into a dish of strawberry ripple ice cream.

By the time she left The Zany Crowe's Nest, Lorraine felt sick with anxiety. Their mother had demanded to know the reason for the row. But Lorraine had not mentioned the guitar and Gary did not mention Danny. In the face of adult authority, an unspoken, uneasy truce existed between them. As a punishment, neither would be paid any wages for their day's work.

Lorraine was breathless when she reached the square, where she had arranged to meet Joanne. She thought about last night and felt swamped in waves of guilt. Joanne, Amanda and Marian were perched on the back of a bench, their legs resting on the seat. They fell silent when they saw her and she knew she had been the subject of their conversation.

"How's Danny?" asked Amanda in a sweet, enquiring voice. Marian trailed the toe of her shoe along the bench slats.

"How should I know?" Lorraine replied, trying to meet Joanne's eyes.

"I saw you last night." Amanda put her hand over her mouth and gave a stifled giggle. "The two of you. Standing at your bedroom window. My mother thinks it's disgraceful that you're left alone to run wild at night."

"I *don't* run wild. How can you spread such stories about me?"

"I got Robbie to ask Danny. He admitted that he was over in your place last night." Marian, who was going with Robbie, tut-tutted disapprovingly and laid a hand consolingly on Joanne's arm.

"That's typical of Danny Kane. Boasting again," said Amanda.

"But we weren't doing anything!" Lorraine burst out. "We were just looking for something."

"In your bedroom?" drawled Amanda. "Now, whatever could that be?"

"Oh, shut up, all of you," said Joanne. "I haven't got time to hang around here listening to stupid gossip." She pushed Marian's hand away, jumped down from the bench and, with a reproachful look at Lorraine, walked swiftly away.

"Amanda Bell, you are a thoroughbred bitch!" declared Lorraine.

Amanda shrugged. "All I did was tell Joanne what I saw." Her eyes glittered with self-righteousness. "It's only fair that she should know what's what! I *wasn't* telling lies."

"You never tell lies. Yet you always seem to make trouble for people. I wonder why?" Without waiting for a reply, Lorraine walked away.

"Wait, Joanne! I want to tell you what happened."

Joanne kept her head down and did not slow her pace. "I'm not listening to any more of your lies. No wonder you never have any friends. You let me go on with all that rubbish about fancying Danny Kane and the two of you were going together behind my back all the time. And he can shove his group. I've more important things to do with my time."

She tossed her fringe out of her eyes and stared coldly

72

at Lorraine. "I don't want to speak to you ever again. When I choose friends, I like to be able to trust them. That's what I did with you, Lorraine Crowe, and you were lying in your teeth all the time."

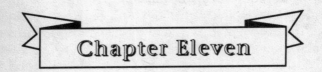

Chapter Eleven

Danny rang The Zany Crowe's Nest and asked to speak to Gary. He was ordered abruptly off the line by Mrs Crowe, who said that staff members were not allowed to take personal phone calls. Robbie called for him as he was replacing the receiver.

"You don't look like a man who touched down on heaven last night." Robbie gave an enormous grin and sighed enviously. "I heard all about it."

"Heard what?" Danny was hardly listening to him.

"About you being over in Lorraine Crowe's pad last night."

"How did you know that?" Danny was surprised.

"Amanda Bell saw you."

"She would."

"She said you were in Lorraine's bedroom. Is that true?"

"What's she suggesting?" Danny could not stand Amanda Bell and her nose for gossip. The suggestive things she said about people always made them feel defensive.

"Oh, you know Amanda." Robbie shrugged. "She loves to gossip." He gave Danny a sly, sideways look. "*Were you?*"

"For a few minutes, that's all. And you needn't grin like that. It's not what you're thinking." He told his friend about the lost guitar.

Robbie didn't believe a word of it. He had heard Amanda Bell's story and it sounded far more interesting.

In Fountain Square that evening, Amanda remarked that the night had a thousand eyes.

"They still couldn't compete with your eyes, Amanda," Danny snapped back and she uttered a high, guilty shriek of laughter.

"Gary told me to give you a message." Jason Cole spoke with the self-important air of one relaying messages from a king. "He's on his day off tomorrow and he'll see you here. He doesn't like the stories you've been spreading about him."

"Tough! Just tell him he'd better bring my guitar along."

"I wouldn't get in his way," warned Jason. "He's mad as hell over you and his sister carrying on." He made a fist-in-the-air sign and nudged Danny. "What's she like? Does she give? Huh? *Does* she?"

"Get lost!" Danny hated the leering grin on Jason's face.

"My mother says it's the quiet ones you have to watch," said Amanda, enjoying her role as witness to the scene. She fussed over Joanne as if she was recovering from a malignant disease. Lorraine Crowe did not appear. When he asked Joanne if she had seen her, she turned away from him and said, "We're not hanging around together any more." She also told him she would not be singing in Dancing on Grey Ash. Her showbusiness career would be moving in a different direction.

"Excuse me!" he said, unable to understand why she was dishing out the deep freeze treatment and refusing to admit that anything was wrong.

When Gary swaggered into Fountain Square the following day, Robbie saw him first. "There's that creep. If he took *my* guitar, I wouldn't let him get away with it!" The words were a challenge.

"I'm going to smash his face in," declared Danny in a hollow voice.

Robbie cupped his hands to his mouth and hollered, "You're for it, Crowe. Danny Kane says he's going to smash your face in if you don't give him back his guitar."

Danny made a gulping sound and tried to swallow. One part of his body poised to flee, the other part poised for battle.

"You tell him, Danny!" His friends surrounded him, shouting encouragement and thumping his arms.

"Tell me what, Kane?" Gary stood belligerently before him.

It was impossible to remember the music that had filled them with such energy and excitement. He jabbed his fist at Danny's face. "I know what you were really up to on Saturday night. My sister's very upset over you and your lies."

Voices broke their concentration for an instant when a group of girls approached the square.

"What's happening?"

"It's a fight."

"Let's have a look."

"Stupid dorks! They're always fighting."

"Hey, it's Danny Kane."

Danny heard the surprise in Joanne's voice. But he was charging at Gary, his fists swinging and hitting flesh. The group of boys crowded around, yelling encouragement. Gary hit back. He was solid and muscular, stronger than Danny and more skilled at defending himself. Danny hit the ground. The surface of the paving slabs scraped his face. He did not know how many times he fell. But his anger lifted him back to his feet each time.

"Lay off him, Gary!" Robbie sounded nervous.

"Shut your face!" ordered Gary. He was kneeling on Danny's back, twisting his arm.

"You're looking desperate, Dan," Jason laughed loudly. "Desperate Dan!" he repeated for the crowd's benefit. "Now that's a *dandy* joke." He thought he was absolutely hilarious. But no one laughed with him.

Danny panted. His arm felt as if it was on fire. His nose began to bleed. He could taste blood in the back of his throat. He gagged when he tried to swallow. The arm-lock tightened.

"Let go of me. You'll break my arm," he yelled.

"Not until you admit that you tried to pin that stupid story on me. There was only one reason why you were in my sister's room and it had nothing to do with your guitar. Go on, admit it!" Gary roared in his ear. "Say it. Say 'You're right, Gary. I'm a liar!'"

"No! I *won't*!" There were bubbles of blood on his face. The boys drew back, embarrassed by the mess, the pain in Danny's eyes.

"Say it!" Gary repeated.

Danny began to sob. "You're right…I'm…I'm a liar!"

"I told you," said Amanda. "Didn't I tell you, Joanne?"

"Leave him alone…you'll break his arm…leave him

alone!" Joanne was crying, swinging her fists at Gary.

He released his hold on Danny's arm and glared at the crowd.

"I told you! There never *was* any guitar! Never! Never! Never!"

He dashed his hand over his eyes and ran from the square.

"The Boil is coming!" A warning growl from Robbie distracted them. Mr Boylan, the park keeper, was hurrying across the grass, looking very officious and menacing.

"What's going on here?" he demanded.

"Just a bit of messing, Mr Boylan, sir," said Robbie. The boys hid Danny from view. "We're demonstrating a few karate moves."

"Any fighting and you lot are out on your backsides," said the park keeper. He glared suspiciously around and sniffed, as if trying to track down the source of trouble. A little man with a mouth as tight as a clenched trap, his reputation for controlling the youth of Beachwood rivalled that of Sergeant Hilliard. When he disappeared through the shrubbery in pursuit of a dog without a lead, Robbie helped his friend to the fountain. Danny washed the blood and dirt from his face. The young people drifted homewards. No one could think of anything to say. The cold water stung his face and washed it clean. But Danny knew that nothing, not even six spurting jets of water, would ever wash away his shame.

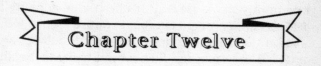

Chapter Twelve

The envelope dropped through the letterbox. Lorraine opened it and took out a plain white card with the word *Tart* written in red all over it. The previous day someone had sprayed paint on the wall at the back of Oaktree Estate: "Danny Kane gets it from Lorraine Crowe." It was two weeks since the night Danny came to her house and she had never realised it was possible to be so miserable.

Her brother had fought with Danny. He had stood before her with his hands on his hips, his head jutting forward. "That poser, Danny Kane, won't bother you any more," he had said, demanding her attention.

She ignored him and carefully turned a page of her book.

"He admitted telling lies about the guitar. Everyone in Fountain Square heard him and they all know what he was doing in this house."

She looked up from her book. "You're pathetic, Gary! As usual, you're just trying to make trouble. I know

Danny Kane. He's not like that." When her eyes continued to challenge him, he was the first to turn away.

The following day she had seen Danny in Beachwood Village. His face was bruised and there was an ugly red graze on his cheek. He bent his head, not stopping to speak to her or even pretending to notice her.

Jason Cole had rung her at the end of the week and wanted to know why she did not come to the square any more.

"I'm not interested," she said, shortly.

"You're right. It's kids' stuff. Would you like to come out with me some day? We could go for a walk in the park and have pizzas afterwards." She was surprised. Jason was Gary's shadow, someone who used to tease her and laugh at her. He had made a fool of her in Fountain Square. Her knee was still scarred as a result. But on the phone he sounded so grown-up. As he tried to persuade her to change her mind, his voice was balm on her misery. "I'd be too embarrassed to go," she finally admitted. "People have been spreading stories about me."

"Don't pay any attention to that garbage. They'll be talking about someone else next week." Jason blamed Danny Kane and hated the things he was saying about Lorraine.

"What things?" She felt sick.

"Never mind. I know they're not true and that's all that matters. Come out with me. Show him that you don't care what he says."

"I'm sorry, Jason. I can't." After she hung up, she went upstairs to her bedroom and sat on the edge of her bed wondering where her newly found confidence had gone.

The colourful girl in the portrait seemed to mock her but when she gazed upon the painting for a long, quiet time, realising that every tiny brush stroke, every dash and splash of colour was a thought, a decision, an image in John Donaldson's mind, she grew calm again. Her days were spent reading and doing chores around the house. She walked Candy along the coast road and called into John's studio. If he was busy painting he would wave her into an armchair and she would silently watch him at work. Sometimes he cursed loudly, chewed his beard and stomped up and down the studio muttering fiercely to himself. Even in the midst of his most hysterical behaviour, she was comfortable with him. She listened while he tried to explain what it was he was trying to express in his painting. As a boy he had been frightened of the dark and he wanted to paint a picture of a dense black cloud in which his childhood fears would appear, full of mysterious and suggestive shapes within the blackness.

"I want to make visible the invisible horrors that a small child senses in the darkness, yet I don't want them to be seen, only hinted at," he explained. "Does that make sense to you?"

"It's as clear as mud," she replied and began to understand why his beard was like a nibbled bun and her vocabulary of swear words increased at an alarming rate every time she visited White Light Studio. When he showed her the painting, she stared for a long time at the canvas. In her mind music was strumming faintly, lullabies in the darkness. She gave a startled cry and covered her face.

"What is it?" asked John Donaldson.

"Nothing!" She would not cry. It had never made her cry and she was not going to start now.

"Tell me what you saw? Please." He made her sit down

and waited until she was calm again.

"The night my father came into my room to say goodbye. He did not turn on the light. How could I have known he was not coming back? I was only four years old. He held my hand so tightly that it hurt. But I didn't cry. Afterwards I heard my mother cry. I've never been able to see his face since then. Maybe if he'd turned on the light!"

She stood up, abruptly pushing away the artist's hand.

"I think your painting is going to be very good," she said in a prim little voice and left the White Light Studio with its black shadowy images. When she returned the following day, John Donaldson was working furiously, his face tense with concentration. But Lorraine refused to look at his painting.

Jason Cole continued to ring her. One day, he was waiting for her outside The Zany Crowe's Nest, where she had gone for her lunch. He swung into step beside her. On passing the entrance to Hobourne Park he pleaded, "Let's just go for a short walk?" He put his arm casually around her shoulders.

She hesitated, tired of the empty house and the phone that never rang with a call from Joanne. It was a bright, blustery August day and she wanted company. She wanted to feel special. Danny Kane was walking along the narrow path that skirted the park. When he saw Lorraine, he stood perfectly still. He opened his mouth to say something. She put on her snootiest expression, walked past him and entered Hobourne Park with Jason.

The leaves were at their most magnificent, richly green and arching above them. They walked along Pine Trail, a meandering narrow path, thick with a soft carpet of pine needles. High, thin trees stood like soldiers on each side and the air was fresh with the clean smell of pine. It was a dim and private place, a much-favoured trail for young couples.

Lorraine felt awkward walking alongside Jason, especially when he kept his arm around her shoulders. He told her about his interest in rugby and the keep-fit routine he worked on each day, starting with a swim in the Beachwood Leisure Centre at seven in the morning. She told him about the books she liked to read. He said he had never read a book in his life, apart from the rubbish he was forced to read in school. This sounded like a boast to Lorraine. She was beginning to feel very bored. Why had she agreed to walk with a bone-headed dork who could talk about nothing but rucks and scrums and rugby tackles? The path narrowed even more. Lorraine squirmed uneasily and offered to walk ahead. Jason pushed closely against her. His arm felt heavy and tight. When he pulled her around to face him, she turned away and his kiss connected with her hair.

"Ah, come on, Lorraine. I've wanted to get off with you for ages."

"No! Leave me alone." She tried to pull away from him.

He closed his two arms around her and held her in a loose but firm grip. Again he moved his face towards her.

"No!" She was getting angry. "I don't want to!"

"Then why did you agree to come with me?" he challenged her. "You know the score."

"What score? I agreed to go for a walk with you because you kept pestering me. I don't want to kiss you. So, just stop it, Jason."

"That's not what you said to Danny Kane!" He was

beginning to get angry.

"I wasn't up to anything with Danny Kane," shouted Lorraine.

"That's not what he's saying. The word is out that you're a tart. So, don't pull the frigid bit on me, Lorraine."

She pushed him away and began to run.

He called after her and she ran faster, hearing his footsteps behind her.

When Stinger Muldoon with Beethoven on his lead came around the corner, she narrowly avoided crashing into him. But Jason ran full tilt into the bald-headed man and almost knocked him over. The bulldog began to snarl and lift his tail. Despite being on a lead, he still had the power to terrify. Jason turned pale. He backed off, apologising. Stinger loosened the lead and Beethoven crawled on his belly towards him. Jason uttered a high groan of fear and stopped, afraid to move in case the dog fell upon him. Beethoven barked loudly. After a sharp command from Stinger, he continued to look ferocious but made no attempt to attack. Suddenly Lorraine wanted to laugh. "Beethoven is as big an actor as his master," she thought. "He's loving every moment of this."

"Is this little punk giving you trouble?" Stinger asked.

She nodded, enjoying the sight of Jason's contorted expression. "Only a little," she replied. She had completely forgotten that the sight of Stinger had once sent her running hysterically from Beachwood Strand.

"Then let him say he's sorry. Are you ready to say you're sorry, little boy?" asked Stinger.

Jason was furious. But his terror was stronger than any other emotion. "I'm sorry, Mr Muldoon."

"*I* didn't ask for an apology," scoffed Stinger. "It wasn't me you offended."

84

The dog edged nearer. His eyes glistened. He had long yellow teeth and the meanest eyes Jason had ever seen.

"I'm sorry, Lorraine," he muttered.

"Say it nicely. Say it with feeling," ordered Stinger.

Jason kept a wary eye on Beethoven. The dog had reached his toes. He ground out another apology then, at a sharp command from Stinger, fled thankfully from Hobourne Park.

"You're very kind, Mr Muldoon," said Lorraine.

"Indeed I'm not," said Stinger, as if she had offended his fearsome reputation. "I just hate scummy little boys. But Beethoven likes them, especially for his evening meal."

Lorraine smiled. "I'm sorry for running off on you that day on the beach," she confessed. "I didn't realise that you're really just a great big softie."

"Don't you dare spread rumours like that!" Stinger ordered. "I've worked hard on my reputation and I don't want it ruined by a daft girl with daft notions." When he smiled his face wrinkled like a deflated football.

But when Lorraine left Hobourne Park and said goodbye to Stinger, she allowed her anger to roll back over her. She kept hearing Jason's words: "The word is out that you're a tart. So, don't pull the frigid bit on me, Lorraine." She hated Danny Kane. She would never forgive him for twisting the time they had spent together into a boastful lie that had broken her friendship with Joanne.

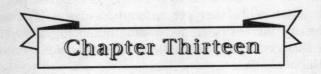

Chapter Thirteen

When Caro asked her brother when he was going to form Dancing on Grey Ash, he stared blankly at her and muttered about having more important things to do. Then he did nothing at all. Caro had heard about the fight. She had also heard the gossip surrounding it and had told Amanda Bell that her tongue would be more useful to society if she used it for spreading manure instead of spreading lies about other people. Amanda had been furious, especially when Joanne said, "How very true," in her most sarcastic voice and walked home from Fountain Square with Caro.

"Come in and say hello to Danny," ordered Caro. "He's in rotten humour all the time."

But he had not wanted to talk to Joanne. When Caro tried to discuss what had happened in Fountain Square, he told her to "get knotted" and mind her own business.

His younger sister sulked, hurt that her efforts to be nice to him were having no effect. "You're just a big fat pain. To think that I organised a fan-club and a protest demonstration for you. I must have been nuts!"

He felt ashamed of his behaviour but was unwilling to do anything about it. Every time he thought about the fight, he winced. How could he have given in to Gary Crowe? He felt like a coward and a wimp, believing that that was how everyone else saw him. He had forgotten the pain and the panic, the sensation of blood clogging his throat and the fiery, tearing sensation in his arm. All he remembered was that one moment of weakness.

His mother was furious over his lost guitar which had been a gift from his parents one Christmas. After the fight, she had pressed a packet of frozen peas against his cheek and threatened to call on Mrs Crowe. She was a tolerant and easy-going woman but became tigerish if any of her cubs were put upon. Danny begged her not to interfere.

"I'm almost sixteen," he said. "I can't have my mother running out and fighting my battles for me. I'll sort it out myself."

She reluctantly agreed to let him handle it his own way. "His way" seemed to be a prolonged period of sulking in his room, snarling at the family members, refusing to see his friends and lying prone in the darkened lounge watching daytime television. Finally, she lost her temper and ordered him upstairs to clear out his bedroom.

"I'll do it tomorrow," he promised. He had been making that promise since the start of the school holidays.

She flung the curtains open and he blinked as sunshine flooded the room.

"Recognise it?" she asked, sarcastically. "It's called daylight. Now get upstairs and start working!"

There was something about her voice that penetrated Danny's self-pity. He knew this was not the time to argue.

Upstairs in his bedroom, he set to work. He was an addicted hoarder, unable to throw out anything that had once held his attention, no matter how fleetingly. Six large black plastic sacks later, the room was beginning to look normal again. He was also in much better humour. He discovered a box of football cards, collected from cereal packets when he was six.

Where had the years gone, he wondered? If they kept going so fast he'd soon be an old man with wobbly legs. When Joanne entered his room, the cards were spread over the floor and he was busily organising the players into their correct teams. Danny realised that he was delighted to see her.

"Don't throw me out or I'll bite!" She held up a warning hand and flopped on his bed. It squeaked, protestingly. "Let's bounce up and down on the bed and drive your mother mad," she suggested. Her impish grin had returned. They had done this once before and Mrs Kane, unable to ignore the sounds of bed springs creaking suspiciously from her younger son's room, had rushed up the stairs with a sweeping brush in her hand, determined to beat the two of them out of the room. She had been unable to see the funny side of the joke but they had laughed for hours afterwards. Now, they smiled uneasily at the memory and Joanne stopped bouncing.

"As it's a woman's privilege to change her mind, Danny, I just wanted to let you know that I'm ready to resume my position on the Dancing on Grey Ash line-up."

"There'll be no lead guitarist if I ever *do* get around to forming it." He frowned at her. "Not that you believe a word of that story," he muttered. "You're as bad as Amanda Bell."

"Don't say that." Joanne shuddered. Her face clouded with misery. Then they began to talk. It was just like old times, the words spilling out, interrupting each other, finishing each other's sentences, knowing each other's thoughts. Or so it seemed until Joanne told him why she had gone through a very mixed-up stage.

"I believe I was suffering from a disease called 'delayed puberty,'" she stated, half-amused and wholly embarrassed.

"I can't believe you'd fancy *me*!" Danny felt very flattered as well as astonished.

"There's no accounting for bad taste," she replied, tartly. "Fortunately, bad taste can always be improved and in my case that is what has happened."

Danny hugged her. "I'm glad you're better. I'd hate to lose my best mate."

Joanne groaned, theatrically. "You have *such* a way with words, Danny."

The attic was converted into bedrooms for his sisters so Joanne had to help him carry the bags down to the garden shed. This small building was suffering from severe overcrowding.

"I'm going to have to hire a rubbish skip and shift this lot," said his mother. "Otherwise the walls will collapse outwards."

The rubbish skip! It was so obvious, so simple, that he could not understand why he had not thought of it until now. The rubbish skip in Lorraine's garden had been filled with rubble from the kitchen extension. He had stared down upon it in that last instant before she had pulled the curtains on her bedroom window. Could his guitar have been dumped into it? The fleeting thought became a certainty. His guitar was buried somewhere beneath the heap of concrete blocks and broken wood. It was now the third week in August which meant that the builders had returned to work on the extension. He knew there was no time to lose.

The van with Larry Walsh, Building Contractor, written on the side was parked outside Lorraine's house. There was no sign of the rubbish skip. Nor was there any answer to his ring on the doorbell. Danny dashed around the side entrance.

"The lad's at work and your little girlfriend's gone for a walk with her dog." Larry's nose was peeling from too much Spanish sun. His stomach sagged over his jeans and his bare top half was mahogany brown.

"Where's the rubbish skip?" gasped Danny.

"That's gone as well, " said Larry. "We managed to get it loaded onto the lorry about half an hour ago."

"Where's it going?" Danny was almost dancing with impatience.

"It's gone to Baymeadow Dump. What's the problem, son?"

But Danny had no time to reply. Bent low over the handlebars of his mountain bike, his legs pumping the pedals, he was speeding towards Beachwood Village.

Baymeadow was a sprawling landfill operation, located two miles to the north of Beachwood. Eventually the County Council hoped to turn it into a public park. Until then, it was a dumping ground for rubbish, a feeding ground for rats and seagulls.

Danny cycled through Beachwood Village and out along the coast. The heat spell was continuing. Cars were parked on each side of the road and children splashed in the sea. Sweat trickled down his face. His shirt stuck to his back. The winding coast road seemed endless, a twisting up and down ribbon of tar that would eventually lead to Baymeadow. He noticed the bus stop with its glass shelter. Someone had shattered the glass the previous night.

The pieces had been swept up but, in the sunshine, splinters glinted like diamonds strewn across the road.

At Harbour Bend, he saw Stinger Muldoon smoking a pipe and standing at his front gate. The walls of his cottage were studded with cockleshells. Beethoven lifted his heavy head, barked a welcome but was too lazy to move from his comfortable sprawl in front of Stinger.

Suddenly Danny's bike began to wobble. Without looking down, he knew that a splinter of glass had lodged in the front tyre. He groaned and slumped over the handlebars.

"Ah, Danny boy. What ails you on such a fine day?" Stinger strolled over to him.

"Did you see a rubbish skip go by?"

Stinger scratched his head. "A big, ugly yellow yoke?"

"That's it. How long ago?"

"It's a while ago."

"I'll never catch it now." In despair, Danny looked down at his flat tyre. "It's going to Baymeadow and I think my guitar is in it."

"Danny Kane without a guitar. Unthinkable! Just let me get the old jalopy and we'll try and catch it."

Stinger's van smelled of fish. Beethoven nuzzled the floor appreciatively as he settled down in the back among the stacked crates that Stinger used to pack fresh fish for delivery to the village fish shop and The Zany Crowe's Nest. Danny opened the side window and breathed, deeply.

Seagulls wheeled above Baymeadow. The dump was

surrounded by a high wire fence. A smoke-screen of smouldering rubbish darkened the sky.

Stinger drove through the gate. Danny bounced up and down in the front seat as the van jerked over the rutted tracks. He saw two men talking beside the yellow skip that fitted snugly on the base of a lorry. One of the men swung himself into the driver's cab and pulled a lever. The skip began to tilt.

"*Stop!*" yelled Danny. He was out of the van in a flash and sprinting towards the mound of foul-smelling rubbish that loomed above the truck. He waved his hands frantically. Stinger beeped the horn and Beethoven howled.

"Holy magnolia! What's all the fuss about?" demanded the driver.

Danny cupped his hands and shouted up at him, "Don't dump it yet. I've got to check something!"

The driver stopped pulling the lever. The skip ground to a standstill then swung back into position again. Springer gave Danny a heave up the side. He moved cautiously over the loose rubble which grazed his shins and threatened to twist his ankles. Within a few minutes, he spotted a dust-covered narrow shape jutting between two planks of wood. His heart skipped with excitement, as he gently eased away the wood and saw the body of his guitar case. He whooped with joy, forgetting, in his delight, that Gary Crowe had deliberately stashed his guitar in a rubbish skip with the intention of its being buried out of sight, forever. Kneeling on a flat slab of concrete, Danny opened the guitar case. His body stiffened with disbelief when he lifted the instrument free. Its strings had been broken. A knife had carved deep fissures across its wooden face.

He ran his hand helplessly over the damaged wood. He was angry, a sizzling feeling that seemed to run like a wire from the top of his head to his toes.

"Why did you do it, Gary?" he kept whispering. "Why?"

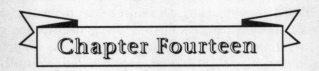

Chapter Fourteen

When Lorraine brought Candy for her daily walk along the coast road, she saw Danny Kane cycling past. He was wearing shorts but he looked flushed and hot. He did not notice her. She strolled over the warm sand and climbed Shale Head. Candy panted and dived into the rolling sea. The rocks were a warm bed and Lorraine turned her face to the sun. Last night, she had slept fitfully, weeping often, her face buried in her pillow in case her mother heard her.

She had not meant to listen to the conversation between her mother and John Donaldson. But the sound of a car door slamming at midnight had woken her and she had recognised the deep tones of the artist. He must have been dining at the restaurant. She often wondered about the relationship between her mother and John. Since separating from her husband, Mrs Crowe had never displayed any interest in another man. Once, when Lorraine said it was very unfair that divorce was not allowed in Ireland because if it was her mother could marry John, Zena Crowe had drawn her eyebrows up and looked at Lorraine in astonishment. She said that Lorraine was far too young to be thinking about things like that and divorce was of no concern to her because she did not intend to marry again, ever. "Once bitten, twice shy," she said with the distant smile she always displayed when forced to talk about unpleasant things. As for John Donaldson, she had drawn her eyebrows up even further in astonishment, he was a family friend, nothing more.

Gary had dashed up the stairs and slammed his bedroom door. The two adults entered the lounge. Lorraine wanted to show John where she had hung his painting. When she reached the lounge door, she hesitated. It was not fully closed and she could hear her mother talking about Gary. Mrs Crowe sounded weary. Since his father's guitar had been confiscated, he had been sullen and unresponsive. Jack, the chef, was threatening to resign if she did not remove her son from the kitchen. Lorraine wanted to sneak back to her bedroom. But she was afraid they would hear her if she moved.

"Wanting to have something belonging to his father? Was that such a terrible crime?" asked Mr Donaldson.

"Yes! Jeff was a weak and selfish man. Why should he have such a claim on Gary's love when he did so little to earn it?"

"He is Gary's father. There's blood between them, no matter what happened afterwards."

"He deserted us, that's what happened afterwards!"

"The children *need* to talk about their father, Zena. They need to understand what happened between the two of you. I worry about this silence you have imposed on them. It has affected them, you know."

"I don't know anything of the sort! I have given them everything they need, security, love, a comfortable home, a sense of…"

The words stopped and Lorraine heard a light thudding noise, as if knuckles tapped on glass, thudded angrily against the portrait of her mother. "Look at you. Perfect Zena Crowe. I painted you as you wanted to see yourself. But you are not a portrait, Zena. There are things you have to see. Things like your son, half you, half Jeff. And those two halves make him into an individual. Gary is not responsible for how he looks or the memories he brings back to you. No matter how bitter you feel, he is not responsible for your past. As for Lorraine—"

"Are you suggesting that I have a problem with Lorraine?" she interrupted.

Lorraine felt panic. She wanted to shout: "Don't talk about me. I'm listening." But something, curiosity, fear, anxiety, she did not have a name for the feeling, held her prisoner, listening to John Donaldson's words.

"She's always been a shadowy little thing, smack bang in the middle between you and Gary. Neither one of you has ever noticed how she feels. When she achieves good results, you don't congratulate her. Instead, you use it as a stick to beat Gary, to show him how much better he could do if he tried harder. And he reacts by being jealous of her, by belittling her whenever he gets the chance. Why do you think she wanted to go to boarding school?"

"Iona Abbey has an excellent academic record. Lorraine wanted a challenge—"

"She wanted a chance to be herself. And that's what she has done. I've seen her confidence grow. But she still finds it impossible to talk about her father. She wants to please you so much that she has closed her mind to the past. I think she should visit Jeff and get to know him again. It might help her to come to terms with what happened."

Lorraine was shivering in the hall. She wanted to weep. Then, as clearly as the portraits John Donaldson had painted of herself and her mother, as clearly as the fear she had felt when she looked into the night shadows in his latest painting, her father's face appeared from within a dark, secret place in her mind.

"He won't make me cry. He never has and he never will," she whispered, fiercely.

"I won't have the past dredged up to upset them." Dimly she heard her mother reply to something the artist had said.

"But that's just the problem, Zena. The past! You can't let go of it and I don't think I can live there any longer with you."

"Have you finished minding my own business?" demanded Zena Crowe. "If so, then I would like you to leave."

"Is that what you really want?" he asked, sadly.

"No, it's not!" Lorraine answered silently, remembering the night she had used the same harsh tone on Danny.

"Yes! And I would prefer it if you did not return," replied her mother. Lorraine wanted to fling her arms around her and take the hurt from her voice.

Without caring whether or not they heard her, she stumbled up the stairs to her room. Her bed was cold, so cold. Cold tears on her cheeks. It took her a long time to stop crying. She drifted into sleep, feeling like a lost child who had trespassed briefly on adult time. She cried again as she lay on the rocks. Salty tears that slid thinly from the corners of her eyes. The sun was so hot. A shadow fell across her. Opening her eyes she saw a blur of legs.

She sat up and grabbed her towel, pretending to wipe the perspiration from her face.

"I recognised you from the beach," said Joanne. "Do you mind if I sit down beside you?"

"It's a free country," Lorraine looked down at Candy's sleek head in the water.

Joanne fanned herself with her hand. "This weather! I'm in melt-down. You look as if you've been crying."

"Sunburn!" snapped Lorraine.

Joanne glanced, shame-faced, at her. "I've wanted to talk to you for ages. I'm really sorry about the way I behaved that time when…when…oh, you know what I'm talking about?"

Candy clambered over the rocks and waited until she reached the two girls before shaking herself vigorously over them. By the time she had been ordered to crawl to the far side of Shale Head and commit suicide, the embarrassment between the friends had eased a little.

"I couldn't stop thinking about you and Danny together and all the things I had told you and that you must have been laughing at me behind my back all the time," confided Joanne.

"Do you still believe that?" asked Lorraine, curtly.

"Not for ages. I've wanted to say I was sorry so many times. But I was embarrassed and…and…jealous!"

"Jealous!" Lorraine was astonished. "Why?"

"I knew that Danny fancied you. I could see it from the way he kept looking at you. He never looked at me like that."

"That's rubbish!" Lorraine's cheeks flamed.

"It's not. He told me so this morning. We talked the

whole thing over and we're friends again."

"You told him *everything*?"

Joanne nodded. "Everything. Imagination can play funny tricks at times, especially when we desperately want something. I had created something between Danny and myself that was never there to begin with. So it was only right that I should bury it as well. Danny's friendship is too important for me to throw away."

"Good for you. But he's no friend of mine. He spread that story about me..."

"No, he didn't! That fight with Gary was awful. Danny said he lied about his guitar only because Gary nearly broke his arm in two. Danny's a great musician but Michael Carruth he is not. And now he's so ashamed of himself. He thinks you can't stand him. He actually believes you're going with that creep, Jason Cole. Whatever gave him that idea?"

"I can't imagine," replied Lorraine, blank-faced.

"I told him that you had far too much good taste to bother with that slug."

Lorraine coughed into her towel. "What did he say about...em...?" her voice was muffled.

"He agreed that Jason was a slug."

"No, not that!"

"About fancying you?"

Lorraine was too embarrassed to do anything but nod and listen very carefully to the reply.

"Do you still like him, Joanne?" She looked anxiously at her friend. "I never wanted him to come between the two of us! Friendship is important to me as well."

Joanne looked very grown-up for a moment until she relaxed, grinned and threw out her hands to embrace the sea and the high rocks of Shale Head. "I'm going to be a singer. A megastar. How can I fit men into my life at the same time? He's all yours, dar-ling." The last word ended on an affected drawl and the two girls laughed in that familiar easy way that Lorraine loved so much.

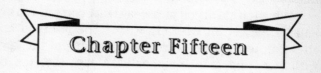

Chapter Fifteen

"I want you to give me back my father's guitar!" Gary stood in the doorway of his mother's office. Receipts and tax forms were stacked neatly on her desk. She was entering figures into a computer and looked up, startled. Her lips tightened. "You know the answer to that, Gary. Now, please leave me alone. I have work to do."

"Please give it back to me. I don't want to play it. I'm going to give it to someone."

"A likely story."

"It's true. I've done something awful and—"

"Gary, you are always doing something awful," she interrupted. "Now will you please go back to the kitchen. That is an order!"

"Why is it that you never listen to me?" He banged his fist off her desk. The neatly-arranged receipts fluttered to the floor. He made no attempt to pick them up.

His mother sighed and folded her arms. "OK Gary, I'm listening. But the answer is still *no*!"

Gary bowed his head. He was unable to look at her. "That time when you took Dad's guitar...well...I was so mad...I...I did something..." His voice trailed away, miserably.

"What is it? Will you please say what you want to say and let me get on with my work." She returned her attention to the computer screen, tapping at the keys with her long manicured nails. A tap, tap, tap of impatience.

"Listen to me!" His head was bent so low that she could only see the top of it. His hair was thick and soft, the colour of corn. Jeff's hair. "I smashed up Danny Kane's guitar. I destroyed it and then because I was so ashamed of myself, I hid it in the rubbish skip."

"What are you saying?" She gasped with shock.

"You heard me."

"But why...why would you do such a dreadful thing?"

"Do you really want to know?"

She had to lean forward to hear him.

"I was so mad at you that I took a knife and carved it up. And do you know what I said to myself while I was doing it? At least this time you won't think I'm like my father. He wouldn't do such a thing because he loved his music more than he loved you!"

Mrs Crowe pressed her hands to her forehead. She was unable to speak. Nor did she look up when her son opened the door and silently left her office.

Gary did not stop running until he reached his house. The builders had left for the evening. In the lounge, he stood before the portrait of his mother. The painted grey eyes reminded him of cold, wet beach pebbles. When Lorraine put her hand on his shoulder, he jerked as if her touch had given him an electric shock.

"What are you doing spying on me?" He spun around to face her.

"I'm not…you look so upset. What's wrong with you, Gary?"

"Nothing!" His face looked blotchy in the stream of sunshine coming through the window.

"Was there a row in the restaurant?"

"What do you care?" he jeered. "You never have any problems. Everything's so easy for you. She *never* fights with you or blames you for being like…like…" His voice broke.

When the doorbell rang, shrill and insistent, it startled them.

"Keep your hair on!" Gary roared but the clamour continued. Lorraine opened the hall door.

"Danny! What's wrong?" She noticed the battered, dusty guitar case he was carrying.

"Is Gary here?"

"Come in. He's in the lounge."

Gary swallowed. His Adam's apple jerked in his throat. He could not take his eyes from the guitar case.

"How did you find it?" he gasped.

Danny did not reply. He removed the guitar and held it towards them. Scarred wood and twisted broken strings. Scratches on the fingerboard were clearly visible. A deep cut in the wood looked like a wound.

"Oh no…oh Danny…no!" Lorraine ran her hand helplessly over the damaged wood. "Did you do this, Gary?" She looked angrily at her brother.

"It was an accident…" The words trailed miserably away.

"I'm going to take you apart." Danny trembled.

Gary knew it was not from fear but from a deep,

hurting anger. Suddenly he was frightened. His mother's portrait loomed behind him. Danny moved closer.

"Get away from me!" Gary lashed out, pushing him away.

"You can't shove me around any more." Danny stood firm before him. His fist lashed out in a movement so strong, so unexpected, that the bigger youth stumbled backwards, his heels hitting the hearth, his head banging against the portrait above the fireplace. It rocked wildly from side to side. He recovered his balance and desperately turned around. His hands tried to stop the swaying movement. The bracket holding the portrait on the wall broke and the painting lunged towards them. Lorraine skipped out of its way, laughing in a shrill unnatural shriek. Gary still held the portrait by its sides, as if his strength would stop the inevitable from happening. But the weight was too heavy. It slipped from his hands and crashed to the floor. The frame split. Glass shattered. When he turned it over, a large glass splinter was embedded in the piercing gaze of Zena Crowe. Lorraine wondered if she would ever be able to stop laughing. Laughing like some crazy hyena, her hands wrapped around her stomach, her head bent. Only it did not feel as if she was laughing and nothing, nothing on earth, would ever make her feel so awful.

"What's she going to say?" Gary looked pathetic, his face crumpled, trying to fit the pieces of glass together as if it was some kind of crazy crystal jigsaw.

They did not hear the sound of a car in the driveway. Mrs Crowe stood in the doorway and stared at her portrait as if the splinters of glass were embedded in her heart.

"Who did this terrible thing?" she asked, softly.

"I did." Danny trembled. "It was an accident…"

"He had nothing to do with it. Leave him out of it," cried Gary. "I broke it."

Danny opened his mouth to protest but at the touch of Lorraine's restraining hand, he stayed silent.

Mrs Crowe knelt down and touched the shattered glass. Her face was hidden from her children as her hands slowly moved over the fragments of her portrait.

"Do you hate me so much, Gary?" she whispered.

Gary knelt beside her. "Don't do that. You'll cut yourself." He turned her hand over and held it tightly. His mother drew in a long shuddering breath. Her eyes looked fuzzy and red-rimmed. The skin underneath was puffy with deep cobwebby lines that he had never noticed before.

"I'm not like him," whispered her son. "I've never stopped loving you."

Zena Crowe bent forward and picked up a shard of glass. "He painted what I wanted to see," she whispered. "What I wanted to be. I thought it would stop me looking back at the past." She tried to smile. Then she stood upright, leaning heavily on Gary's arm. "It's broken, gone. But we're still here, together. We're a family." She stretched out her other hand and touched Lorraine. "All that matters now is that I have my children to help me pick up the pieces."

Danny saw them form a tight and protective circle. He quietly went from the room and they did not notice him leaving.

•••

A week later Gary knocked on Danny's door. "I want to give you this." He held out his father's guitar. "It's yours.

To make up for the damage I did."

"I can't accept that!" Danny was shocked. He held his hands to his sides.

"Please take it. I want you to have it." There was nothing noble or self-sacrificing about Gary's expression. He looked hurt and sad and his eyes were filled with a longing to run fast from Danny with the guitar clasped tightly to his chest. Yet Danny saw his determination, his effort to make amends. He knew it was very important to accept this gift.

"Thanks, Gary. You can come around here and play it any time you want."

"Thanks. I will. John Donaldson was over in our place last night and he gave me the name of a friend of his who's a guitar teacher. I'm starting lessons soon. Maybe I'll have my own group some day. That'll be competition for Dancing on Grey Ash."

"It sure will!" Danny sighed deeply with relief.

The two boys walked to Fountain Square.

"Did you know that my father's coming to Ireland for a visit during the Christmas hols."

"So Lorraine told me. She says she doesn't want to see him."

"I know. But my mother thinks she should."

"So do I," said Danny.

He could see her blonde hair. She was sitting on the white park bench with Joanne. She looked up as he approached. Only a few more days before she returned to Iona Abbey. They had promised to write to each other. But, before she left, there was time to swim once more from Shale Head. To dance to the music of her father's guitar on the sandy red paving stones. To dine in the Pizza Palace and walk slowly through the long and narrow path of Pine Trail. A leaf fluttered from one of the trees. It was deep green with a faint puckered fringe of bronze at the edges. Summer was ending in Fountain Square.

Other Beachwood Titles

The Slumber Party

The Debs Ball

School Bully